S0-BLT-342

"You shouldn't have come out in the dark by yourself, Rachel," Jacob said softly. "The dark can be dangerous."

Leaning down so that her hair brushed against his cheek, she looked into his eyes. "I think the only danger is from you."

He said nothing, merely gazed at her with hypnotic eyes, then reached for her hand. Giving her a lazy smile, he placed her hand on his bare chest. The crisp hair there curled possessively around her fingers. "Ah, Rachel, you shouldn't have come tonight," he said, wrapping his hands around her waist.

"I know." She tipped her head back, baring her throat. The heat of the night pulsed around her, and the heat of Jacob burned through her.

"A Victorian gown." He dragged his hands across her back, pressing the thin cotton fabric so that he could feel the heat of her skin. "You're a paradox, Rachel. A hoyden in pearls. A hot-blooded minx in Victorian white. You still drive me wild. All these years, there's never been a woman who could make me feel like this."

Suddenly, passion and betrayal boiled between them, and his mouth branded hers with fire. . . .

WHAT ARE *LOVESWEPT* ROMANCES?

They are stories of true romance and touching emotion. We believe those two very important ingredients are constants in our highly sensual and very believable stories in the *LOVESWEPT* line. Our goal is to give you, the reader, stories of consistently high quality that may sometimes make you laugh, sometimes make you cry, but are always fresh and creative and contain many delightful surprises within their pages.

Most romance fans read an enormous number of books. Those they truly love, they keep. Others may be traded with friends and soon forgotten. We hope that each *LOVESWEPT* romance will be a treasure—a "keeper." We will always try to publish

*LOVE STORIES YOU'LL NEVER FORGET
BY AUTHORS YOU'LL ALWAYS REMEMBER*

The Editors

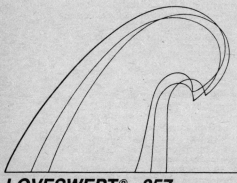

LOVESWEPT® • 357

Peggy Webb
Higher than Eagles

BANTAM BOOKS
NEW YORK • TORONTO • LONDON • SYDNEY • AUCKLAND

HIGHER THAN EAGLES

A Bantam Book / October 1989

LOVESWEPT® and the wave device are registered
trademarks of Bantam Books, a division of
Bantam Doubleday Dell Publishing Group, Inc.
Registered in U.S. Patent
and Trademark Office and elsewhere.

All rights reserved.
Copyright © 1989 by Peggy Webb.
Cover art copyright © 1989 by George Tsui.
No part of this book may be reproduced or transmitted
in any form or by any means, electronic or mechanical,
including photocopying, recording, or by any information
storage and retrieval system, without permission in
writing from the publisher.
For information address: Bantam Books.

*If you would be interested in receiving protective vinyl
covers for your Loveswept books, please write to this address
for information:*

Loveswept
Bantam Books
P.O. Box 985
Hicksville, NY 11802

ISBN 0-553-22019-5

Published simultaneously in the United States and Canada

Bantam Books are published by Bantam Books, a division
of Bantam Doubleday Dell Publishing Group, Inc. Its trademark, consisting of the words "Bantam Books" and the
portrayal of a rooster, is Registered in U.S. Patent and
Trademark Office and in other countries. Marca Registrada.
Bantam Books, 666 Fifth Avenue, New York, New York 10103.

PRINTED IN THE UNITED STATES OF AMERICA

O   0 9 8 7 6 5 4 3 2 1

*For Belden's intrepid
eagles in the sky,
Kenneth and Jerry Webb.*

Prologue

Rachel looked good in black.

Jacob drew his coat collar up against the chill and leaned against the solid oak tree, watching her. She stood proud and elegant, her honey-colored hair twisted into a chignon and her eyes wide and green under the bit of black hat that dipped over her forehead. A single strand of pearls gleamed against the stark black of her dress.

The wind caught her scent and blew it across the packed red clay and cold stone markers. Roses. Rachel always smelled like roses.

Jacob felt as if someone were twisting a knife in his gut, probing the old pain that had been with him for six years. He'd thought he could put Rachel behind him. Heaven knew, he'd tried. The Middle East, South America, China, Africa—he'd been to them all, courting danger with the abandon of a man who had lost paradise and had no hope of regaining it.

But now, seeing Rachel beside the open grave, he

knew that she would never be merely a part of his past. She was a flame inside him that refused to be extinguished.

Jacob bit back a sound that was part curse, part anguish. He almost turned to go, but the dull sounds of earth hitting the casket held him. Rachel was burying her husband, and now she was free. Free to love and betray again.

The wind picked up, howling over the gravestones, as the small gathering of mourners began to disperse. She was walking in his direction, her head turned toward the gray-haired man who held her arm—Martin Windham, her father. Jacob remembered him as a ruthless man whose pleasant social manners camouflaged an iron will. He hadn't aged much in six years.

But then neither had Rachel. She looked as fresh and elegant as she had when he'd first met her.

Suddenly she saw him. Her face went white, and her eyes widened. She spoke to her father briefly. There seemed to be a quiet argument between them, then Martin turned and strode angrily in the direction of a parked black Mercedes. Rachel hovered beside the open grave a moment, then she lifted her chin in defiance and came slowly toward Jacob across the now-deserted cemetery.

He wasn't prepared for the impact she had on him. Standing before him, tall and elegant, she made his heart race. He braced himself against the tree.

"Jacob."

He died a small death when she spoke his name. As always, her voice was soft and musical, like a symphony whispering through pine trees.

"Hello, Rachel." He pressed hard against the tree, fighting the sweet memories aroused by the fragrance of roses, cursing the weakness that had sent him flying to Biloxi.

"Why did you come?"

"To offer my condolences."

Rachel twisted her hands together, then abruptly put them behind her back so Jacob wouldn't see the effect he was having on her. After six years he still made her quiver inside. Guilt slashed through her. She'd just buried her husband, for pity's sake. She had no right to be reacting to another man, even if that man was Jacob Donovan.

"How did you know?"

"I was in Greenville when it happened. Apparently Martin had it printed in the paper."

"He would. He loved Bob."

Did you? Was it love that drove you to his bed not two months after I left the country? Jacob wanted to ask. Instead he studied her, his gaze burning over her as if he could probe the secrets of her heart. Even in the feeble light of the January sun, Rachel radiated that special fire that had once warmed him, that particular glow that set her apart on the stage.

"Are you still singing, Rachel?"

She felt something jolt inside her. Once Jacob had known everything about her—what she was thinking, what she was doing, what she was planning. The knowledge that he no longer knew saddened her. And yet, she thought, it was not surprising. Jacob would not have kept up with news of her, would not have known that she had records on the top-ten chart, that she was in great demand as a nightclub performer—not only in Mississippi but throughout the United States. No, Jacob Donovan had too much pride to hold onto something that was no longer his. And besides, he had no interest in music; his love was flying.

And yet . . . he was there, bronzed and bold and brash and altogether too real. A small chill ran along her spine. Whether it was due to an old passion she'd tried to forget or to fear, she didn't know. And she dared not question it.

"Yes. I'm singing. But not lately, not since Bob's first heart attack."

"Rachel." He reached out as if he wanted to touch her cheek. His hand hovered there in the air between them, the sun glinting off the sprinkling of red hairs, gleaming on the flat, squared-off nails.

Rachel's skin tingled, as if he had actually brushed against it.

"I'm sorry," Jacob said, drawing back from her. The tree trunk seemed to steady him.

She knew he was talking about the death of her husband, but she couldn't keep from thinking of the past. They'd been so much in love, inseparable from the moment she and her father had moved to Greenville. She was an up-and-coming singer, and Jacob had just completed his law degree. Then, without warning, he'd joined a fire-fighting team that specialized in oil field fires. He'd quickly gained fame as one of their most intrepid troubleshooters. The dangers inherent to his profession became overwhelming for her. When he'd been called to an oil field fire in Saudi Arabia, they'd quarreled bitterly. Two months later she had married Bob Devlin, her manager.

Rachel studied him. He still wore danger and charm with equal ease. And he still made her heart turn inside out.

"I'm sorry too," she whispered.

Around them, the wind moaned and the old iron gate creaked as Martin approached. But neither of them noticed. They were caught up in each other. A flame sparked in the center of Jacob's blue eyes. His cold expression thawed.

He bent down and took her lips quickly, before he could change his mind. His hands caught her shoulders and his mouth claimed what had been stolen from him six years earlier. He felt her brief resistance, then the sweet flowering of her lips as she responded to him. It was a small victory, but it gave him no pleasure. Instead it served to deepen his pain.

He jerked his head back and stared down at her, watching a thousand emotions play over her beautiful face. The last was shock that they could kindle such passion in the chilled atmosphere of death.

"Good-bye, Rachel."

Jacob turned and walked away while he still could, leaving Rachel among the tombstones, leaving her to break some other poor fool's heart.

Rachel watched him go, then turned and joined her father. Martin's black Mercedes transported her along in a cocoon of comfort and quiet to the big white house that looked out over the Gulf of Mexico, the house she and Bob had shared for the last two years. She walked into the polished hallway and stood listening to the sounds of silence.

She had no idea how long she stood there, but suddenly the silence was broken by a low, droning noise, the unmistakable sound of an airplane. Instinctively Rachel ran onto her columned front porch and looked up.

An old World War II fighter, a P51 Mustang, roared over her house. It was Jacob. She knew. For unlike him, she had kept up. She'd known precisely when he'd purchased the expensive antique. He was flying hard and fast, cutting through the sky, soaring higher than eagles, just the way he'd always said he would.

She shaded her eyes against the sun and watched until he was out of sight.

"Good-bye, my love," she whispered, then, turning, she went back into her house.

One

Biloxi was sweltering in June.

Jacob, who could have been cooling himself in any mountain resort in the world, told himself he was there to visit the fly-boys at Keesler Air Force Base. He wanted to caress the turbo props, run his hands down the sides of the military jets, feast his eyes on the tankers.

He had just returned from Maracaibo, where he and his specially trained team had extinguished one of the biggest oil field fires in the history of his career. He'd courted danger once more and won, and he felt good.

"That Devlin woman is singing tonight at Louie's. Man, what a looker." Captain Mark Waynesburg squinted into the sun as if seeing a vision, then turned his attention back to Jacob. "A group of us are going. Want to join us?"

"Rachel's singing again?" Hearing her referred to as "that Devlin woman" sent a shock wave through

him. She used to say, in some of their more intimate moments, that she'd been born to be a Donovan.

"You know her?"

"Yes. I know her."

"Then you'll come?"

Jacob rammed his fist in his pocket and started
to refuse, but his basic honesty asserted itself. Wasn't
Rachel the reason he was in Biloxi? He'd spent the
last six years running from the truth, but the time
had come to face it. He would never be free of Rachel
until he knew why she had jilted him for another
man.

"Count me in," he said.

Mark clapped him on the shoulder. "She's the
best singer ever to hit this town. You won't regret
it."

He already did. The last time he'd seen Rachel, she
had been standing beside her husband's grave. Six
months ago. And even then, he couldn't keep his
hands off her. What would it be like this time?
Knowing she was free? Knowing that nothing stood
between them? Nothing except misunderstanding
and betrayal and guilt and six lonely years, he reminded himself. Dammit, he'd go. He *had* to go.
Seeing her again was the only way he could learn
the truth, the truth that would set him free.

Rachel saw him at the back of the audience—Jacob
Donovan, his hair like flame, his eyes so blue, they
looked like twin pieces of sunlit sky, even in the
smoky dimness of the nightclub.

Only her training kept her from missing a beat,
saved her from forgetting the words. As she crooned
the Jerome Kern love song, she watched him lean

forward in his chair. Nothing showed on his face—
not love, not hate, not guilt, not longing. To the
casual observer he appeared to be just another man
enjoying her music. But she knew better. He was
Jacob Donovan, the great pretender. And now that
he was in Biloxi, she had to be on her guard.

She finished the song and left the stage to wild
applause. Backstage she paced, praying he would
leave, praying she would never have to face him
again.

Jacob stayed for her second show. His compan-
ions had gone, but he was there, slouched low in his
chair, twirling a half-empty glass in his hands, his
gaze riveted on her.

She tried to avoid looking directly at him, but in
the middle of "The Man I Love" her eyes sought him
out. Old habits die hard, she thought. She had never
sung that song without thinking of Jacob Donovan.
Now she could no more resist looking at him than
she could deny her own name. Her stomach quivered, and her hand tightened on the microphone.

"Why are you here?" she wanted to scream. Instead, she kept on singing.

By the time she finished her show, the club was
empty except for Jacob and a couple of teenage
lovers. Par for the course on a Tuesday night, she
thought.

She hurried to her dressing room, anxious to be
away from the searchlight of those bluer than blue
eyes. Her hand was on the zipper of her gown when
she heard his voice.

"Hello, Rachel."

She whirled around. He was leaning against the
door frame, his face unreadable, his eyes as cold as
glaciers.

Her hands faltered on the zipper. "Jacob." She gave him a brief nod, and tried to maintain a professional distance. "Did you enjoy the show?"

"I didn't come back here to talk about the show."

"Why did you come?"

Instead of answering, he left the doorway and moved into the room. His eyes raked her from head to toe, and then she saw the flame leap in their depths. That look of pure passion evoked memories so powerful, she had to catch the back of a chair to steady herself. She remembered Jacob in the sunlight beside the river, pressing his bronzed body into hers; Jacob with hay tangled in his red hair, his eyes crinkled with laughter; Jacob waking in her bed, reaching for her and telling her she was the wind beneath his wings.

Her tongue flicked over her dry lips, and she stood so still, she could measure the exact rhythm of Jacob's footsteps as he stalked her.

When he was only inches from her, he stopped, pinning her to the spot with his intense gaze. She pressed a hand over her heart as if to calm its fluttering. The silence stretched between them until she could almost hear the air crackling with tension.

At last he spoke.

"You always did need help with your zippers, Rachel."

She held her breath as Jacob gently turned her around. Goose bumps popped out on her arms.

"Do I make you nervous?" Lifting her heavy hair, he dragged his fingertips lightly across the back of her neck.

"No." Her shiver mocked the lie. She wanted to scream; she wanted to run. But she could do nothing except stand and wait for the hot pleasure of Jacob's touch.

"Black becomes you, Rachel."

"Thank you." She could barely speak above a whisper, for now his hands were on the back of her sequined gown. The metallic hiss of the zipper was loud in the charged quiet of the room.

"Are you still in mourning?"

His strong, blunt fingers were on her bare skin now, trailing fire in their path. Her reaction was so strong, so unexpected, that for a moment she thought she had been transported back in time. A lethargy stole over her, and she tipped her head back on her limp neck.

"No," she whispered. The room seemed to spin, and nothing existed for her except Jacob and the ecstasy of his touch. "Yes, oh, yes."

"Awww, Rachel." Jacob turned her easily, sliding her dress over her shoulders as he pulled her into his arms. He bent over her, his breath hot against her skin.

"No," she whispered. But it was too late. Both of them knew it was too late.

His mouth slammed down on hers, and her eager response thrilled them both. She molded her body to his, trying in one desperate moment to wipe away the six years that had separated them.

His mouth roused her almost to the point of frenzy. She felt ripe, full to the bursting point. An aching longing filled her.

"Oh, Jacob," she murmured against his lips.

In answer to her plea, his mouth left hers and roamed down the side of her neck. He planted fierce kisses at the base of her throat, moved downward and seared the tops of her breasts. Hauling her closer, he fitted her hips close to his.

She was drugged by him, drowning in him. Another moment of this insanity and she would be lost. There would be no turning back. "No. Oh, no." She pressed her face into his shoulder. "Please, Jacob."

He lifted his head and looked deep into her eyes. "Please what? Please do or please don't?"

The remoteness in his voice chilled her. *How could love had grown so cold?* she wondered.

"Please let me go."

He pulled her dress back onto her shoulders, walked away, and straddled a chair. The small room vibrated with his presence. Across the tiny space that separated them, she could still feel his body heat.

Turning her back to him, she sat at her dressing table and picked up the nearest thing she could find—her hairbrush. Anything would serve to calm her shaking hands. Glancing up, she saw his reflection in the mirror. There were laugh lines around his eyes that hadn't been there six years before, and fine lines of stress bracketing his mouth. He looked more bronzed, more solid, and more dangerous, as if being in constant peril had toughened him.

"I let you go a long time ago, Rachel."

She dragged the brush through her hair, taking her time before answering. She had to do it right; she had to send him away from Biloxi.

"I let you go," he continued, "the day you betrayed me by marrying another man."

Her control snapped. She whirled around on her stool and shook the hairbrush at him. "I betrayed you? If I remember correctly, you had a choice, and you chose to live in constant danger rather than with me. You left me, Jacob. I didn't leave you."

He was shocked at her intensity. "I didn't leave you, Rachel. I went to Arabia on business. As I recall, I asked you to go and you refused."

She closed her eyes, willing herself not to dredge up the past. Nothing would be accomplished by doing so.

"Yes, I did. I refused." She faced the mirror again and began brushing her hair. "It's over and done with. Let the past stay buried."

She shivered as his bold gaze raked over her. The air seemed to pulse between them, heavy and electric with emotion.

"I'm not here to relive the past."

"Then why are you here, Jacob?" She laid the hairbrush on the dressing table and turned to face him with quiet dignity. "After all these years, why are you here?"

"I have to know the truth."

All the color drained from her face. Jacob half rose from his chair.

"Rachel? Are you all right?"

"Yes." She lifted her hands and pressed them against her hot cheeks. "It's the pressure, I suppose. Death leaves so many loose ends."

Jacob felt the anguish rise within him. He needed no more reminders that for the last six years Rachel had belonged to another man, had kissed another man, had slept in another man's bed. He willed himself to sit calmly in his chair.

"I'm sorry, Rachel. It must be hard for you."

"Yes." She smiled at him, grateful to be off the subject of the past.

"It doesn't show. You look wonderful."

"So do you. You must thrive on danger."

"I always did, Rachel."

They were treading on shaky ground again. She decided to steer them to a safer topic. "And how is your family?"

"Well and happy and growing."

"I hear your twin sisters, Hallie and Hannah, are both pregnant again." Jacob arched one quizzical eyebrow, and she added, "Dad would never discuss the Donovans, but my friend Evelyn Jo keeps me informed."

So, she cared enough to keep up on news of his family. The thought pleased Jacob so that he threw back his head and laughed.

Rachel joined him. It felt good to laugh again—especially with Jacob. But then, everything had always felt good with Jacob.

"Hannah takes great pride in saying that she started it this time. Their daughters were born only two weeks apart."

"I know. I envy them." She made herself remain calm as he studied her.

"You and Bob never had more children."

It wasn't a question; it was a bomb dropped into the silence between them. Rachel folded her hands carefully in her lap and looked at a spot on the wall behind Jacob's head.

"You kept up?"

"No. Someone told me about your son . . . Mom, I think. She's a hopeless romantic. She thought I still cared."

"You don't, of course."

"No."

Rachel looked him straight in the eye, but she

couldn't read his careful expression. She could only hope he was telling the truth.

"No, we never had more children."

"You used to say you wanted a big family."

"Bob was older." She watched his face, praying he would believe her. "One seemed to be enough."

Looking at her with her long honey-and-butterscotch streaked hair and generous mouth, Jacob held on to the absurdly jealous thought that Bob had been too damned old to perform more than one miracle. He even hoped that fathering one son had tuckered him out so much, he'd had to spend the next six years celibate, recovering.

"Did you love him?"

Rachel's head went up in defiance. "I married him, Jacob. That's all that matters."

"No. It's not all that matters." He stood up abruptly and kicked aside his chair. "When I went to Saudi Arabia, I left behind a woman I loved, a woman I fully intended to marry. I want to know what in the hell happened."

She rose to face him, regal in her rage. "What happened is that you and I fought over your bull-headed determination to do everything in the world you could to put yourself in danger. You seemed bound and determined to get yourself killed, one way or the other—in one of your damned fast planes or in some godforsaken part of the world fighting an oil field fire. I couldn't go through that again."

"I think we've had this conversation before. Are you going to let your mother's untimely death rule your emotions for the rest of your life?"

"Untimely death!" She stabbed the air with her finger for emphasis. "Hers was a foolhardy death, one that never would have happened if she hadn't been taking dumb risks in that air show, flying that old World War One plane with no more thought than she would have had flying a kite."

"And so you wrote me a Dear John letter because of your mother." His face was unreadable as he strode across the small space. "I don't believe it, Rachel. We'd fought over my profession before. It was a difference we could have worked out." He gripped her shoulders. "What in the hell happened while I was gone? What sent you running to Bob Devlin's bed?"

Jacob was a worthy opponent, but Rachel was more than a match for him. She'd be damned if she'd be intimidated or dominated by Jacob Donovan. And she certainly had no intention of ever telling him the truth.

Her eyes flashed fire as she squared off with him. "Love. Is that what you want me to say, Jacob? That I loved him?"

"Dammit, did you?"

"Yes . . . I loved him." She felt no triumph at the pain she saw in Jacob's eyes. But she'd endured pain too. Six years of it. And guilt, besides. But it was a small price to pay for sanity. She looked straight into Jacob's eyes and sent home the last barb. "He was always there for me—and he was damned good in bed."

Jacob loosened his grip. He began slowly caressing her bare shoulders. She felt his power, his turmoil, and his tremendous magnetism.

She toughened her mind even as her body began to go slack in his hands.

"You'd have me believe you couldn't wait to climb into another man's bed." His hands continued their massage. Every nerve in her body was screaming for release. "After all we'd been to each other, all the

promises we'd made, you want me to think you
changed your mind and fell in love with somebody
else—in two months time."

Suddenly, the caressing stopped. Jacob released
her and stepped back. "I don't believe you, Rachel."

She crossed her arms in front of her and gripped
her own shoulders. They were still warm and tin-
gling from his touch.

"Let it go, Jacob," she whispered. "Please, just let
it go."

"I'll never let it go until I learn the truth." He
turned and quickly left the room.

The sudden silence thundered around her. It would
have been so easy, she thought, just to give in to
him. But she had her son's future to consider.

"Never," she whispered fiercely. "You'll never learn
the truth."

Only three people knew, and one of them was
dead.

Two

Jacob found her house Wednesday afternoon.

It was the kind of house he'd always imagined Rachel would live in. The tall white columns and wide verandas were cool and elegant, just like their owner. Huge live oaks, draped with Spanish moss, guarded the front lawn, and a white fence protected the house from the busy boulevard that faced the gulf.

Rachel, in white shorts and halter top, was kneeling beside a bed of bright red petunias.

He stood at the gate, enjoying a stolen moment of watching her unobserved. Her legs were as long and luscious as he remembered, the here-to-eternity legs of a tall woman. And her skin was that special honey hue of blondes who spend just enough time outside to let the sun kiss them.

Jacob found himself getting nostalgic, remembering the good times they'd had. He remembered the exact texture of that golden skin, soft and satiny with an underlying firmness. He remembered how her eyes would darken from spring green to jade when he touched her.

Impatiently, he rammed his fists into his pockets. Hell, he thought, if he didn't watch himself, he'd be so carried away by his Irish sentimentality, he'd forget that Rachel Windham Devlin had cast him off like an old shoe. Clenching his jaws together, he strode toward her. If he'd known how fierce he looked, cocky and arrogant and solid and dangerous, silhouetted against the fiery sun, he'd have been pleased. Jacob, like all the Donovans, loved to make an entrance.

"Rachel." The way he called her name was a command not a greeting.

Her head jerked up. Jacob had to give her credit. Except for the widening of her eyes, she seemed totally in control, royal even. He wanted to lean down and kiss that imperious look right off her face.

He stood over her, feet planted apart, blocking out the sun. "Doing a little gardening to ease your conscience, Rachel?"

She jerked a handful of weeds out of the ground before answering. "My conscience doesn't need easing, Jacob Donovan."

"Yes, it does. For all those lies you told me last night."

Rachel grabbed at her flower bed again, but this time she came away with a handful of petunias. Oblivious, she flung them aside like so much crabgrass. "Nobody invited you here, Jacob Donovan. Go away."

"Not until I get what I came for."

Another handful of flowers bit the dust. "There is nothing here for you." She swiped angrily at her cheek and left a trail of dirt. Damn Jacob Donovan for coming, she thought. She used to see him, standing just the way he was now, feet apart, looking for all the world like he'd conquered the universe, and she'd go limp with wanting. And now, six years later—she sneaked a peek at him—now, it was just as bad.

Madder at herself than at him, she snatched another handful of petunias and flung them into the dirt.

"Go away and leave me alone."

"I'll never leave you alone, Rachel." He knelt beside her and stilled the hand that was hovering over another clump of flowers.

"Don't touch me."

She tried to jerk out of his grip, but he held her fast.

"Make no mistake, Rachel. It's not you I want."

Her heart slammed so hard against her ribs, she thought she would faint. Jacob's next words restored her sanity.

"I want the truth," he continued.

She saw a way out and took it. "You want the truth about why I jilted you?"

"Yes."

"Then I'll tell you. I didn't love you enough, Jacob. I was too young. What we had was puppy love." She forced herself not to waver under his stare. "The truth is I never really loved you."

The smile he gave her was the most dangerous thing about him. "Is that why you're mutilating your flower bed? You're tearing up your flowers over a man you never even loved."

She thrust out her chin. It was smudged, too, he noticed. He came dangerously close to kissing her. Instead, he laughed.

"Rachel, you are the worst liar on the face of the earth. You always were." He released her and reached for an uprooted petunia. "You are also a bad gardener. Here, let me help you fix this flower bed."

All she wanted him to do was go. She felt as if a hurricane had blown in off the gulf, and she was standing right in the eye. She snatched the poor wilted flower from his hand.

"Give that to me. My flower bed is no concern of yours."

"Everything you do is my concern, Rachel. Don't you know that?"

"Why? If you don't want me, for heaven's sake, why?"

He picked up another flower and took his time patting it back into the rich black earth. "Everywhere you go, I'll be there. Every song you sing, I'll be listening. Every move you make, I'll be watching. I'll dog you from here to the ends of the earth until I learn the truth." He sat back on his heels and took his time viewing his handiwork. Then he turned to her, and she felt as if she were looking into the blue-hot fires of a furnace. "It's the only way I can ever be free of you."

She felt chilled, even in the ninety-degree heat. "You really mean that, don't you?"

"It's a promise, Rachel."

She lost control with him, just as she had the night before. Losing control had always been so easy with Jacob. "I won't have it." She snatched a handful of petunias out of the ground and flung them at his chest, dirt and all. "Who do you think you are to come barging into my life after six years?" She reached down again and came back with only a clump of weeds and soil. It didn't matter. She drew back her hand and watched with satisfaction as the whole dirty mess drifted over him. She was getting as soiled as he, but she didn't care. She simply wanted to get him out of her well-ordered life. "I won't let you ruin everything I've worked for. I won't let you!"

"Rachel." He caught her hands as she aimed another chunk of dirt at him. She struggled, and she was almost his match. Tall and slim, she was just one inch shy of Jacob's five ten.

They rolled together in the dirt, and she hit him with every weapon she had, knees, elbows, fists, feet.

"Stop it, Rachel." He pinned her beneath him. The breath whooshed out of her.

"No. Dammit, Jacob Donovan. Let me go."

"Not until you calm down."

She wriggled a fist loose from his grasp and aimed it at his ear. It missed by a city block.

He chuckled. "If you're going to take up street fighting in your old age, you'd better get a few lessons."

"Damn you."

Still laughing, he kept her pinned down. "You used to say you wanted to be a Donovan because you admired the Irish spirit. Show me your Irish, Rachel." He leaned closer and got a whiff of her fragrance. His laughter ceased. He tucked a lock of hair behind her ear. "Rose perfume to garden in?"

The unexpected tenderness of his voice made her stop struggling. "You always did put your perfume in the most provocative places. Where is it now, Rachel?" He nuzzled her ear. "Here?"

He smelled like soap and mint toothpaste and freshly turned earth as he explored her.

"Or here?" His lips touched the based of her throat, right where her pulse was doing a crazy fandango. "Here?" His voice was hoarse as his tongue traced a hot line across the tops of her breasts.

She fell in love all over again with the man she'd never stopped thinking about for six years. His audacity, his boldness, his wicked good looks, his Irish temper, his great boom of Scottish laughter, even his recklessness—all caught her up on the same giddy merry-go-round she'd known when she was twenty-three.

He lifted himself on his elbows and looked down at her. There was no laughter in his face now. What she saw scared her.

"Rachel?"

"No, Jacob. I'm not a wide-eyed innocent anymore. I don't believe in fairy tales. Let me go."

For a second, she thought he was going to release her. Then his face hardened. "And I'm not Prince Charming anymore." He caught her hands, pinning them above her head. "I'll let you go, but first I have to find out just how much you never loved me."

He caught her to him fiercely. His mouth was demanding. It possessed, it punished. And it was impossible to resist. As hard as she tried, she couldn't make her body verify the lies she'd told him.

When he was finished with her, he lifted his head.

"You kiss like a hungry woman, Rachel. Are you?"

She added one more lie to her web of deceit. "No. I'm merely an experienced woman, Jacob. Six years of experience, as a matter of fact."

His hands cupped her face, his fingers pressing so hard, she knew they would leave prints on her cheeks. But she didn't care. Jacob had already left his mark on her, a mark she would never be rid of.

"I don't need any reminders that you married another man."

"I did, Jacob. You can't change the past."

He leaned close, studying her as intently as if he were committing her features to memory. She thought he was going to kiss her again, but suddenly he released her. He stood up and walked quickly across the lawn and down the brick path.

He strode through the gate without ever looking back.

She dusted the dirt off her shorts and went back to her flower bed. Only when she heard the plane in the sky did she realize she was crying. When she shaded her hand over her face to look up, she felt the tears on her cheeks.

"You can't change the past, Rachel Devlin," she told herself. But as she watched the World War II plane circle, she wished she could.

Flying had always made Jacob feel free.

But not today. No matter how fast or how high he flew his P51 Mustang, he still felt like a Christmas box that had been flattened and thrown out with the trash.

Served him right, he thought. He'd rolled Rachel in the dirt as if she were a common tramp. He'd manhandled her and fought with her. What in the hell was wrong with him anyway? All he wanted to do was to get the two-timing woman out of his life.

Then how come you get all heated up every time you see her? He ignored the voice of his conscience. Sarcastic little bastard. Banking the plane, he turned back to fly over her house again. There was no mistaking it. Set on a wide expanse of lawn, it shone like a gleaming jewel. Whatever else Bob Devlin had done, at least he had kept Rachel in style. Jacob supposed he should be grateful to the man.

Abruptly he pulled back on the throttle and shot high into the sky, higher than eagles. But the sense of freedom eluded him.

When he landed, he went back to the Broadwater Beach Hotel and called his office.

His specialized fire-fighting team was headquartered in Greenville now. When he'd first become a trouble-shooter, he'd been part of a team based in Nashville. After Rachel had jilted him, he'd formed his own team, basing them in Dallas near where his brother Tanner lived. He hadn't wanted to remain in Missis-sippi, because everything about the state had re-minded him of Rachel. Through the years, as Rachel and her manager-husband had moved all over the country—Seattle, San Francisco, Chicago, and fi-nally Biloxi—there had been no reason not to move his business back home.

And so he had.

"Rick, how are things on the home front?"

"Is that you, Jacob? Let me turn down the radio."

Jacob grinned. Rick McGill would be leaning back in the old cane-bottomed swivel chair, sipping an orange soda straight from the bottle, his feet propped on the scarred desk, his blond hair looking as if it hadn't been combed in two days, listening to his favorite radio station, WOLD, the station that spe-cialized in golden oldies.

He could hear the scrape of Rick's chair, the sound of his boots against the tile floor. At the other end of the line the voices of the McGuire Sisters faded into the background.

"I'm back. What's up, buddy?"

"I'm still in Biloxi. There are a few things down here I need to take care of."

"Not to worry. Jack's servicing the equipment, and Mick's giving the Learjet the once over. The rest of us are sitting on our fannies thinking about those sweet little numbers down in Maracaibo."

"Take it easy. All of you deserve it. And let me know if anything comes up."

"I will . . . wait a minute. That's the Lennon Sisters. Let me turn them up." The swivel chair squeaked loudly, footsteps tapped across the floor. "Man, that Kathy Lennon is something else."

After Jacob hung up, he showered, changed, and went to Baricev's for a huge dinner of red snapper. He'd fully intended to catch Rachel's show, just as he had promised, but their afternoon encounter had shaken him more than he liked to admit. He wasn't ready to see her again so soon.

After dinner, he changed into jogging shorts and raced along the gulf, running himself into exhaustion so that he could fall into bed, too tired to think about Rachel. He needed time to get some perspective. He'd deal with her tomorrow.

By the next evening, when she hadn't heard anymore from him, Rachel thought Jacob had given up and gone home.

She should have known better, she told herself. There he was, standing in the shallow water, gazing up the beach. Those stubborn Donovans never gave up. She dragged her feet in the sand, slowing her jogging pace almost to a crawl. She briefly considered turning around and going back to the house, but she knew that wouldn't stop him. Nothing would.

She knew the precise moment he spotted her. His head came up, and his whole body tensed. Finally he started toward her, walking at first, then jogging, then sprinting, spewing the white sand up behind him. In the sunset, it looked like a plume of fairy dust.

The fairy tales she read to her son came to mind, but she was too old to believe in fairy tales. Jacob could never be hers again. No amount of longing would restore things to the way they had been.

"How did you know I would be here?" she asked when he stopped in front of her.

"I gambled, Rachel."

"Gambled?"

"Yes. You're a creature of habit; you like to take a good, hard run before a performance. The beach in front of your house seemed the logical place."

"So you've found me. What now? More questions?"

Instead of answering, he reached out and touched her hair. She stood very still as he lifted the heavy strands and let them sift back through his fingers.

"While I was reading your Dear John letter, do you know what I thought about?"

She closed her eyes, wanting to shut him out. But his image seemed to be stamped on her eyelids. Taking a deep, steadying breath, she dared a look at him. "What did you think about, Jacob?"

"The way your hair looked in the sunset, Rachel. Gold with touches of fire. And the way you smelled. Always of roses." He leaned close, smoothing her hair back from her face. Abruptly, he stepped back. "The memories were enough to drive a man wild."

"I'm sorry it had to be that way, Jacob."

"Are you?"

"Yes. An ocean separated us. A letter was the only way."

"Couldn't you have waited? What difference would a few weeks have made?"

"I couldn't wait." *For reasons you'll never know,* she thought. "I thought that what I had to do was best done quickly."

"And callously. Dammit, a *letter*, Rachel! I had no way of defending myself."

She lifted her chin. "Are we going to fight again, Jacob? If we are, tumble me quickly in the sand, because I have an eight o'clock performance."

Jacob looked at her the way he used to, in admiration tinged with amusement. She squelched the quick surge of hope that tried to spread through her.

Suddenly he laughed. "I hope Bob Devlin appreciated the feisty side of you."

She grinned. "Not the way you used to. He preferred docile women to hell raisers."

"Then he must have been a fool." Quickly contrite, Jacob put his hand on her arm. "I'm sorry, Rachel. He was your husband. I have no right to speak ill of the dead."

She covered his hand with hers. She'd always thought one of the most endearing things about Jacob was the heart-tugging innocence of his quick apologies. "It's all right."

She caught a brief flash of tenderness on his face before he pulled his hand away. "Don't be sweet to me, Rachel."

"Why?"

"It makes me forget."

"Forget what?"

"That I don't love you anymore."

Standing there in the sunset, she longed to wrap her arms around him and beg, "Love me, Jacob. Love me." But she knew that would be insane. Instead, she waited with all the dignity and self-possession she could muster.

Jacob's piercing blue eyes caught and held hers as a thousand memories flooded back. Overhead a sea gull cried out to its mate, then drifted away over the water.

"Don't you, Jacob?" she whispered.

"If I loved you, Rachel, I would show you in a thousand ways." Jacob reached out and cupped her face. "I would touch you"—his thumbs gently massaged her chin—"and kiss you." His mouth covered hers in the briefest, tenderest kisses she'd ever known. "I would hold you"—he pulled her into his arms and buried his face in her hair—"and cherish you."

For one glorious moment, their heartbeats joined. Then Jacob moved away. His arms dropped to his side, and he stepped back. The tide came in and washed between them.

"If I loved you, Rachel, you wouldn't have to ask. You would know."

Jacob turned and walked down the lonely beach.

Three

It was early when Jacob walked through Rachel's gate.

She wouldn't be up yet. He knew, because he'd sat through both her shows the night before. She hadn't finished the late show until two. And she'd looked tired. He hoped his presence in Biloxi had something to do with that. He selfishly wanted her to be losing as much sleep over him as he was over her.

He wanted her to be suffering too.

The gate swung shut behind him, and he walked to her nearly naked flower bed. There were great bare patches where she had uprooted her petunias. Setting his box on the ground, he grinned sheepishly.

He could understand his sleeplessness and his motive for revenge. What he couldn't figure out was why he'd conned the owner of a landscape nursery to open his gates at seven and sell him a big box of petunias.

Still grinning like a penitent schoolboy, he knelt

beside the flower bed and dug a hole for the first petunia.

"What in the world are you doing?"

He looked up, and what he saw took his breath away. Rachel was standing on the front porch, her honey and butterscotch hair tumbled over her shoulders, her green eyes still dreamy from sleep. The filmy pink concoction she was wearing couldn't be called a nightgown and robe by any stretch of the imagination. To Jacob, it looked more like a bit of cotton candy or a pink cloud or even a chunk of heaven that had fallen from the sky.

He swallowed his grin and pinched the head off the petunia he was holding.

"I'm gardening."

She threw back her head and hooted with laughter.

"Unless things have changed, you know as much about gardening as my son."

He tore his gaze away from the enticing vision on the veranda and patted the earth carefully around the broken petunia. Then he started digging another hole.

"Madam, how dare you insult me. I grew up on a farm."

She laughed even harder.

"You're a pretender, Jacob. Your mother once told me that if you had spent as much time with your books as you did thinking up excuses to get out of gardening, you'd have been a genius."

He remembered the time he'd painted himself red, using a leftover bucket of paint he'd found in the barn, and had told his mother he had a rare disease. It took Anna three days to get all the paint off him, and when she did, part of his skin came with it. He'd paid the price with two weeks of irritating pain. It had been the high point of his career in deception.

As he looked up at Rachel, he realized he hadn't come to her house merely to plant petunias. He'd come to see her. He wondered what the consequences of his deception would be.

"That just goes to show you, Rachel. I'm a man of many talents. Pretending is only one of them." He grinned at her. "Want to see my others?"

"No." For the first time since she'd heard him in her flower bed and had impulsively run out of the house, she became aware of her attire. It was not exactly the costume she'd have chosen to face Jacob Donovan in, but it was too late now. She'd just have to make the best of it. She drew herself up regally and tried to pretend her legs weren't weak from longing. "Are you planning to put a flower in that hole?"

He kept on digging. "Yes. Gardening is simple. Just dig a hole and drop the plant in."

"Unless you're digging all the way to China, I'd say the hole is deep enough."

Chagrined, Jacob looked down. Sure enough, he had dug a hole big enough in which to bury a good-sized cat. Rachel descended the steps and came toward him. Suddenly he was smothering in a cloud of pink chiffon and the heady scent of roses. The first consequence of his impulsive decision to plant petunias was upon him; he wanted to pull Rachel into the flower bed and make love to her, right there in the dirt. The intensity of his desire shocked him.

Rachel was a heartbreaker, and he was determined he wouldn't be her victim again. "Would you mind stepping back a little, Rachel. You're blocking the sun."

"Blocking the sun?" She stood where she was, so close, her fantasy nightgown was brushing against his arm and her perfume was turning him to putty.

"Yes, dammit! How can I see to plant petunias when you're in the way?"

"Well, who told you to plant petunias in my garden anyway?"

"You needn't shout, Rachel. I'm not deaf."

"I'm not shouting!"

"Yes, you are."

"Get out of my garden."

He rose to face her. "These petunias are my apology, and I intend to plant them."

"Apology! Don't you think six years is a little too late to apologize?"

He caught her shoulders and pulled her against his chest so tightly, she grunted. "What am I to apologize for, Rachel? Loving you too much? Trusting that you would wait for me so we could work things out?"

"Dammit, let me go. You're just as stubborn and mule headed as you were six years ago."

"And you're just as unbending."

"It's a good thing we didn't marry each other."

"A hell of a good thing."

They glared at each other, panting. The air around them was hot with anger and pulsing with passion.

"Mommy, look!" A small boy burst through the door, his Big Bird pajamas drooping at the waist and a bedsheet flapping around his neck. "I can fly!" The little boy ran to the edge of the porch. "I can fly!" A big black Labrador barked at his heels.

"Benjy, no," Rachel called, but it was too late. Benjy had launched himself off the edge of the porch and was flying straight at them.

Jacob turned and held out his arms. The landing would have been perfect, except that Benjy was coming with such force, he knocked them to the ground. The dog bounded down the steps and circled them, barking.

Benjy bounced up, laughing. "Let's do that again."

Rachel caught him around the waist and hugged her to him. "Young man, how many times have I told you not to fly?"

"Sixty 'leven. Granpa says I'm a beardevil, just like Gramma. What's a beardevil?"

Jacob was enchanted. If he'd had a son, he'd have wanted him to be exactly like the small boy standing in the crook of Rachel's arm. He stood with his sturdy little legs planted apart and his freckled face shining. His eyes were green like his mother's, and his streaked blond hair stood up in front with a cowlick.

His question already forgotten, Benjy turned his attention to Jacob. "Hi, I'm Benjamin Devlin. Who are you?"

"Jacob Donovan."

The little boy stuck out his hand. "Please to meet you, Mr. Donoben."

Jacob solemnly shook his hand. "So, you like to fly, do you?"

"No," Rachel said.

"Yes," Benjy said at the same time.

"Oh, Lordy have mercy!" A large woman bustled through the front door, wringing her hands on her white apron and rolling from side to side with each step she took. "I'm sorry, Rachel. The little scamp got away from me." She made her way down the front steps and across the lawn. When she reached them, she took Benjy's hand. "Now, little mister Benjamin. We'll march right back upstairs and put that sheet on the bed where it belongs. Then we'll get all cleaned up and have a nice breakfast."

Jacob could hardly believe his eyes. Standing beside them was the same woman who had been housekeeper to the Windhams and surrogate mother to Rachel since Mrs. Windham's death, the woman who had once told him she wanted to live long enough to give his and Rachel's children a proper upbringing. He dusted the dirt off his pants and stood up. "Vashti? Vashti!"

"Lordy, Mr. Jacob! Is that you?" She enveloped him in a warm embrace. She smelled like gingerbread and dime-store talcum. "If you're not a sight for sore eyes. Let me look at you." She held him at arm's length. Clucking her tongue, she smoothed back his tousled red hair and wiped at the dirt smudge on his cheek. "Just look at you." Her glance swung to Rachel, who was still sitting in the dirt. "And Rachel too. Turn my back for one minute, and look what happens, the entire household falls apart." Stepping back, she put her hands on her hips. "Now you two just march right inside and wash that dirt off, while Benjy and I put this sheet back on the bed. Then we'll all go onto the sun porch and have a nice, big breakfast."

She didn't wait for a reply. Leading Benjamin, she sashayed back into the house with the air of a woman who knew that her word was law.

Rachel shot Jacob a withering glance. "Don't you dare even consider it."

He gave her an innocent smile. "I'd never dream of leaving you to face Vashti's wrath. If I know her, she'd practically tar and feather you if you sent me away hungry. And with dirt on my face to boot." Still grinning, he leaned down. "Give me your hand, my love. There's no need for you to spend the rest of the day in the dirt."

Rachel knew she'd been outfoxed. She conceded the victory but not gracefully. "All right." Putting her hand in his, she allowed herself to be pulled up. "But don't you dare get any ideas. This is the first and last time you'll be allowed to set foot in my house. And then I want you out of here—out of my house and out of my life."

"There's a price for that, and you know what it is." Turning on his heel, Jacob stalked up her front steps and into her house.

Rachel took her time showering and dressing. For six years she'd felt as if she were in the jaws of a giant trap, and now the trap was closing shut. After she'd dressed, she paced the floor, wondering exactly how she would handle this encounter between Jacob and her son.

Their laughter drifted up the stairs, and she felt sick at heart. For six years her secret had been safe, and now Jacob was here. His mere presence threatened everything she held dear.

She walked to her Louis XIV desk and sat down. Taking a small key, she opened the middle drawer and pulled out a letter. It crackled as she took it out of its envelope.

Her eyes misted over as she read the words she'd written six years ago.

Dear Jacob,
When you left for Saudi Arabia, I wanted to beg you to stay. I almost did. I wanted to pull

you into my arms and bind you to me with the wonderful secret I was carrying. Instead, we quarreled. It's not that I hate your work, Jacob, for I know how you love it. It's simply that I can't bear for our child to grow up with only one parent. I can't stand the thought of putting a baby through the same kind of childhood I had—raised by only one parent, and that one too preoccupied with making a living to pay me much attention.

I'm pregnant, Jacob. I'm carrying your child. Please come back safely so we can make a home for our baby.

It was a letter she had never mailed. The more she'd thought about it, the more she'd known she couldn't face every day not knowing whether Jacob would live through another of those nightmare oil field fires. When Jacob had first signed on with the troubleshooting team, two men had died in an offshore fire in the North Atlantic. Jacob was a daredevil, just like her mother. He took too many chances. She knew she couldn't ask him to give up a job he loved, and she wasn't strong enough to live with the risks.

She'd done the safe, sensible thing. She'd mailed a Dear John letter to Jacob and had married Bob Devlin. He was older, more stable, and he had always loved her—even enough to raise another man's child.

Her plan had almost worked. Life with Bob had been steady and sensible and safe—all the things she'd imagined—and he had been very sweet to Benjamin. But he had not been Jacob. Her decision, however she rationalized it, had deprived Jacob of his son. And she'd borne the guilt alone.

Reaching into her desk again, Rachel pulled out her diary. Flipping back through the pages, she found the one she'd made on Benjy's first birthday.

> I wish you were here, Jacob, to see your son. His smile is so like yours. Though he's only a toddler, he even walks like you, with that cocky arrogant stride that is all Donovan. Oh, Jacob! What have I done?

She turned the pages, skipping to the entries she'd made on each of Benjy's birthdays. They were all addressed to Jacob, and each one brought him up to date on news of his son. It was the only catharsis Rachel had had, for she certainly couldn't have called him on the phone and told him those things. She'd kept her remorse firmly hidden, allowing herself only one day each year to mourn and to confess what she had done—and then only to her diary.

It was too late now. The past couldn't be changed. Taking a deep breath, Rachel locked the letter and the diary back into her desk and started downstairs to give the performance of her life.

They were sitting together at the glass-topped table on the sun porch. Jacob and his son. The two of them looked so much alike, Rachel had to steady herself against the door frame before going into the room. What if Jacob noticed? She had to get him out of her house as quickly as possible.

She sat down at the table and gave them all a false smile. "I'm starving. Let's eat."

Jacob leaned back in his chair in that elaborately

relaxed way of his that fooled most people. It didn't fool her, though. She knew from experience that Jacob was most dangerous when he appeared to be nonchalant.

"What's the matter, Rachel?"

Her back stiffened. "What do you mean?"

"You always bustle when something's bothering you."

"I'm not bustling, I'm sitting in this chair."

Jacob chuckled. "You came into the room as if it were a men-only club and you were leading a parade of suffragettes. You can't fool me."

"Can you fly a suffer jet?" Benjy piped up.

Propping herself on her elbows, Rachel leaned toward Jacob and gloated. "Well, smarty. *Can* you fly a suffragette? We both want to know."

"Not without her permission."

"Chicken."

Rachel then turned to her son, who had been avidly following the exchange. "A suffragette is a name for a special kind of woman who fights for her rights. Later, we'll look it up together in the dictionary, and I'll tell you all about it."

Benjy wrinkled his nose and quickly turned his interest to the hot biscuits Vashti was bringing through the door.

Vashti settled onto the chair beside Jacob, her dress billowing and spreading as her enormous hips pressed against the seat cushion. "So," she said. Her smile left no doubt that she considered Jacob Donovan to be right up there next to Santa Claus and the president of the United States. "What took you so long to come to see us?"

"I've been busy fighting fires."

"I know. Over the years we kept up with what you were doing."

He gave Rachel a triumphant smile. "You did?"

"Vashti did," Rachel lied. She wasn't about to give him any encouragement by telling him that she'd known every time he went to fight a fire—and every time he came home safe.

"Ha!" Vashti's snort said it all. Splitting open three biscuits, she reached for the butter. "Some people I know can't seem to remember things very clearly. Why, there was that time when you were off out yonder in Oklahoma, and we heard over the news that a man had been killed in an oil field fire. I thought she would faint dead away before the announcer ever got around to giving the man's name."

"Did she?"

Rachel ignored the gleam in his eye. "Tragedy makes me ill."

"Ha!" Vashti spread honey on her three biscuits and bit into one with the air of a woman who has had the final word.

Rachel was so anxious to get away from the subject of her interest in Jacob that she made a fatal mistake. "As soon as you've finished your breakfast, Benjy, we'll go to the park."

"Yea!" Benjy bounced up and down in his chair, stopping long enough to grab Jacob's hand. "Can he go too?"

"I'm sure he has other things to do." Rachel shot Jacob a don't-you-dare-contradict-me look.

He ignored her. "I'd love to go. Do you have a ball and bat, sport?" He ruffled Benjy's hair.

"You bet." Benjy jumped up from his chair and started toward the door.

"Benjy," Rachel called. When he whirled back around, she put on her best stern-mother look. "Your breakfast. You hardly ate a thing."

He bounced back to the table, took a big gulp of juice and crammed a dripping buttered biscuit into his pocket. "I gotta get my ball."

When Benjy was out of earshot, Rachel turned her wrath on Jacob. "Your tricks will get you nowhere, Jacob Donovan. You may fool my son, but you can't fool me. I know exactly what you are."

Grinning, Jacob tipped back in his chair. "And what is that, my fiery beauty?"

"You're a crafty, conniving blackguard who will do anything to get what he wants."

"Tell me more, love. I've always enjoyed your temper tantrums."

"Temper tantrums!" Out of control and not caring, Rachel jumped up and dumped her orange juice over his head. "Now let's see who goes to the park."

Jacob roared with laughter. "Do you think a little orange juice will stop me? It just makes me a bit sweeter."

Rachel was astonished by her own behavior. She'd spent six years being a perfectly refined lady. But since Jacob Donovan had been in town, she'd rolled in the dirt and fought and spit like an alley cat.

Still grinning, Jacob wiped at the orange juice with a napkin. "The mosquitoes are going to love me."

Rachel had to smile. Being totally uninhibited felt good; it felt damned good.

"I don't know what came over me. I *do* apologize."

It was the most unctuous and false apology he'd heard, and he was delighted. "How can I resist such a *sincere* apology? You're forgiven, Rachel. And just to show you there are no hard feelings . . ." Jacob's arm snaked out and swiftly pulled her to his chest. Before she could protest, he bent down and took her lips. The kiss was hard and thorough.

Vashti buttered another biscuit. "Looks like old times are here again." She didn't try to disguise her glee.

"Vashti, don't you dare encourage him."

"Well, it appears to me he's doing all right on his own. A man like Jacob Donovan never did need any encouraging."

"You're a wise and wonderful woman, Vashti." Jacob leaned down and kissed her cheek. "Now, if you'll show me the shower and lend me a clean shirt, we can all go to the park."

"Use your own shower, Jacob Donovan." Even as Rachel spoke, she knew it was useless. Vashti was already leading him off toward the shower. They were laughing and talking together like the conspirators they were.

She sat down in her chair and picked up a biscuit. She might as well eat. She'd need all the strength she could muster to deal with that fast-talking Irishman. In spite of the way things had turned out, she grinned. Damn him. He still had charm.

She was into her second biscuit when it occurred to her that she'd better go upstairs and see what was going on. It would be just like Vashti to be turning the entire house over to Jacob. Another thought struck her. Had she left that letter lying on her desk? What if Vashti had let him use the shower in the master suite?

Panic sent Rachel running up the stairs. "Vashti. Vashti!"

At the head of the stairs she almost collided with Benjy and Vashti.

"Lordy have mercy, Rachel. What are you all in a lather about?"

"Where is that pirate?"

"Why, he's in the shower. Benjy and I are going outside to throw a few practice balls while we wait. Is there anything you wanted?"

"Is Mr. Donoben a pirate?"

Rachel patted her son's head. "No, sweetheart, he's a pilot and a fire fighter." Turning to Vashti, she asked, "Which shower?"

"Mr. Devlin's. I found an old T-shirt that we hadn't sent off to the Salvation Army."

Relief made Rachel almost giddy. She gave Benjy a bright smile and a big hug. "Go on downstairs with Vashti, honey. I'll join you in a minute."

As she walked down the hall toward her late husband's room, she could hear Jacob singing.

"Waltzing Matilda, walt-zing Ma-til-daaaa . . ."

What he lacked in talent he made up for in volume. Rachel paused inside the doorway, smiling. Jacob always sang in the shower, especially when he was particularly pleased with himself. That last thought wiped the smile off her face. Jacob had a lot to be pleased about: He'd conned his way into her house and into her shower, and he had neatly cornered her into letting him tag along to the playground. What he wouldn't do was make her run scared.

She jutted out her chin and pushed open the bedroom door. The suite was exactly the way Bob Devlin had left it—neat and orderly, with books organized by category on the bookshelves, the desktop perfectly clear except for a brass duck paperweight, the chocolate-brown puffed comforter unmussed on the bed. On those rare occasions when she'd come to Bob in his bedroom, she'd always had the feeling that no one actually lived there, that Bob was merely occupying a space that wasn't really his.

Now, however, things were different. Rowdy, off-key singing was coming from the bathroom. Funny how that little snatch of song livened up the room, she thought. When she sat in the chair beside Bob's desk, she wasn't aware that she was smiling.

Jacob emerged from the bathroom in a puff of steam. One white towel was knotted around his hips, and he was vigorously rubbing his hair with another. He was midway into the room before he saw her. He stopped singing and gave her a wicked grin.

"I never pictured you in a bed with a brown comforter, Rachel."

"This is . . . was Bob's room, not mine."

"You had separate bedrooms?"

Rachel could have kicked herself. She guessed the sight of Jacob in a towel had unnerved her. Bob wouldn't have been caught dead in a towel. He was always correct and proper, even in bed. Rachel's glance lingered over Jacob's chest, moved downward to the towel.

Jacob's smile broadened.

He'd caught her lusting, damn his charming, roughish hide. She jerked her head around and focused on a watercolor seascape on the wall behind him.

"What difference does it make? I married him. That's all that matters."

Jacob's grin vanished. "Married and living in separate bedrooms." He looked at the bed, then back at her. It was a knowing look. "Separate bedrooms were never your style, Rachel. Remember Gatlinburg?"

Rachel didn't want to remember Gatlinburg. She didn't want to remember anything that would make her want Jacob Donovan more than she already did. But sitting in Bob's austere bedroom, looking at the all-too-delectable man standing before her, she couldn't help but recall Gatlinburg. . . .

Jacob had come back safely from a terrible oil field fire in Texas, and she was between engagements. They had taken a skiing holiday in Gatlinburg. It had been right before Thanksgiving, and all the lodges were booked. They finally found a little inn tucked away in the Smoky Mountains.

"Just got one room," the wizened old man behind the reception desk said.

"One room is all we need." Rachel tucked her hand into Jacob's arm and held on. He was back safely once more, and she didn't want to ever let him go.

"The only problem is the bed." The innkeeper held onto the registration book as if it held state secrets.

"What's the problem with the bed?" Jacob asked.

"It's a twin bed. Barely room enough for a big man like you, let alone the little lady too."

"Rachel?"

"I like to be cozy."

Much later, snuggled together on the narrow bed under the down comforter, Jacob asked, "Is this cozy enough for you, Rachel?"

She put her head on his chest and listened to the steady thrum of his heart. "Hmmm, it's perfect." A vision of Jacob battling the roaring blazes of an oil field fire came to her, and she hugged him fiercely. "I don't ever want to be more than a heartbeat away from you."

He laughed. "You won't."

She squeezed him tighter. "Promise me, Jacob."

"Those are my plans, sweetheart. No separate bedrooms for us. We'll have a great big old king-size bed, just right for romping. Or if you prefer, a twin bed. Just one for the two of us."

Lifting herself on one elbow, she looked into his eyes. "Promise me, Jacob."

"Hey, Rachel." Quick to sense her moods, he tenderly brushed her hair back from her face. "I promise you, baby. I promise."

Content, she put her head on his chest. "Never more than a heartbeat away. . . ."

The words echoed in her mind as she looked at Jacob standing there in her late husband's towel. For a moment she thought that nothing had changed. Jacob had the same powerful body, the same devilish twinkle in his blue eyes, the same wicked smile. Slowly, she rose from her chair and started toward him.

He watched her come. She was everything he'd ever dreamed of, everything he'd ever wanted. The look in her eyes fooled him. He saw the deep intensity, the bright passion that he remembered so well. Jacob was caught in a time warp.

He reached for her. His left hand circled her waist, his right traced her face.

"Do you know how your face glows when you're thinking about lovemaking?"

She said nothing, merely stood in his embrace. She couldn't pull away, not yet. His touch sent shivers through her; the look in his eyes made her weak.

His hands slowly sifted through her hair, cupped the back of her neck, and pulled her closer. Their legs touched, flesh against flesh, hers bare in the brief shorts she wore, and his naked below the towel.

Jacob lowered his head, and Rachel unconsciously parted her lips. Only inches away from her mouth, he hesitated.

"You want me, don't you, Rachel?"

"Yes," she whispered. She saw no point in denying the truth.

His breath was warm against her cheek, his eyes hot and intense. They gazed at each other. Longed. Lusted. The sound of their harsh breathing was loud in the stillness of the room. Behind them, Bob Devlin's bed loomed, a severe brown object that seemed to shout its presence.

"In his bedroom, on his bed . . . you want me."

The sudden coolness of Jacob's tone shattered the spell of passion. She pulled out of his embrace and walked back to the chair. Instead of sitting, she stood stiffly, seeking composure by gripping the back of the chair.

"I got carried away," she said.

"Memories, Rachel?"

"Yes, damn you. Memories." Biting her lower lip, she turned her face away.

He came to her quickly, holding out his arms for comfort.

"Don't." She lifted her hand to stop him. "Don't touch me."

Ignoring her command, he rubbed her shoulder.

"I'm not offering passion, Rachel. Merely comfort for an old friend."

Knowing he would never be hers, she couldn't bear his touch. She jerked away.

"Don't. I don't need your comfort. I don't need anything from you except one thing. Leave. Leave us alone."

"I can't do that, Rachel. And you know why." He strode across the floor, grabbed his pants, and pulled them on. The towel drifted to the floor. There was a small tearing sound as he pulled Bob's too small T-shirt across his broad chest.

"A seam," he muttered. "I'll have it repaired." Lines of tension hardened his face.

"No. The shirt is merely one we missed when we cleared out Bob's clothes. Keep it, throw it away; I don't care. After today, I don't want to see it again."

"Or me. Isn't that what you told me?"

"Yes."

His piercing eyes told her he knew the truth: Every fiber in her body ached to see him, over and over again. She could never get enough of Jacob Donovan.

"I came upstairs to tell you that I won't make a fuss over today—for Benjy's sake. But afterward, I'll move heaven and earth to keep you away from me and my son."

Without waiting for his reply, she stalked from the room. Jacob stood still a few seconds, pondering Rachel's reaction. It seemed to him that her outrage was out of proportion to the problem. He simply wanted to know how the love they'd had could have been forgotten so quickly, how she could have married two months after he left the country. What was she hiding? Why was she so determined to keep him out of her life?

He'd find out. The Donovan men always got what they wanted, and he wanted the truth.

As he left the room, he realized he was following a faint scent of roses. The fragrance made him feel warm inside. He closed his eyes for a moment, remembering the times he'd pressed his face into her rose-scented skin.

"Are you coming, Jacob?"

Her voice, calling up the stairs, brought him out of his trance.

"Coming." The truth, he thought as he caught up with Rachel and followed her out the door, that's all he wanted.

Four

Bayside Park was only four blocks from Rachel's house. It was a quiet neighborhood playground with monkey bars, swings, sliding boards, teeter totters, lots of green grass, and a sand lot for baseball.

Rachel and Vashti sat on a redwood park bench underneath a live oak tree and watched Jacob playing ball with Benjy.

"Isn't that a sight?" Vashti had hardly quit beaming from the time Jacob had intruded into their early morning routine. "He's a natural with kids. Just look at the way Benjy responds to him. My, my. A body would think they were father and son."

Rachel stilled the panic that rose in her chest. Vashti didn't know. And she had no reason to guess. Martin Windham had arranged a very private birth. The small clinic he owned in Mountain City, Tennessee, had been closed to all patients except Rachel when her son was born. Benjamin had been a small baby, just over five pounds, and she had gotten by with telling everyone he'd been born prematurely.

Now, watching Benjamin and his natural father, Rachel decided that only she would notice the way they stood, both of them with feet apart, stocky legs at precisely the same angle. And their hair. Although Benjy's was now blond, more like hers than Jacob's, the glints of red were beginning to show. As he grew older, his hair would darken and turn redder, almost as red as his father's, she guessed. Benjy's cowlick bobbed in the sun. She hoped Jacob didn't remember his own cowlick, tamed now.

"Jacob grew up in a large family," she told Vashti. "You aren't seeing fatherly instincts, you're seeing the little boy that's still in the man. He always did enjoy having fun."

"That's what I always loved about him. Show me a man who knows how to have fun, and I'll show you a man worth having." Vashti pulled a folding fan out of her purse and began to fan herself.

Rachel reached over and patted the old woman's hand. "I know how you loved Jacob."

"You did too."

"Once, long ago. But it's over between us. I don't want you to have any false hopes."

"Ha!"

Rachel knew better than to argue with that one-syllable proclamation. Vashti was as immovable as Big Sugar Mountain. No doubt she knew more match-making tricks than Dolly Levi. Rachel would just have to keep the two of them apart; for if she knew Jacob Donovan, he'd take swift and gleeful advantage of his ally, once he found out exactly how Vashti felt.

"Mommy, look!" Benjy yelled, turning to face the bench, his freckles shining and his cowlick bobbing. "Watch me catch this one."

"Ready, sport? Get your glove up, now." Jacob drew back his arm and aimed a slow pitch at the small boy.

Benjy stuck out his left hand, and the ball landed with a *thunk* in the leather glove.

"That's a boy. Now show me your curve ball." Jacob hunkered down to be on the level of the slow, meandering ball that came his way. When he caught it, he acted as if he were playing with the best pitcher the Saint Louis Cardinals had to offer.

Rachel died a little inside. Jacob *was* a natural with Benjy, she thought. If he ever found out that Benjy was his son and that she'd kept the knowledge from him, heaven help them all!

The ballplayers strode over to the bench, wearing identical grins.

"Mr. Donoben is a great ballplayer. He showed me the curbe ball."

Jacob reached down and tousled the boy's hair. "You're a natural, sport. Got a great left hook." He settled on the bench beside Rachel and stretched out his legs. "I'm a lefty myself."

She tried to keep her face composed. "Lots of people are."

Jacob was stunned by the intensity of her reply. He'd simply been making casual conversation, and Rachel had gone on the defensive. All his instincts were alerted. He said nothing until Vashti took Benjy's hand and led him off to the water fountain. Then he turned to Rachel and nailed her with a fierce blue stare.

"Was Bob?"

"Was Bob what?"

"A lefty?"

"No . . . yes."

"Which one. No or yes?"

"I don't remember."

"You don't remember?"

"He wasn't much for outdoor sports. I guess I don't ever remember seeing him pitch a ball."

"Didn't you watch him write or eat?"

She shifted down the bench so she wouldn't be so close to him. A trickle of sweat ran between her breasts, wetting the front of her halter. She silently cursed the fates for sending Jacob to Biloxi, for making him the kind of man whose mere presence could drive a woman crazy.

"What do you want from me?"

"The truth. Was Bob left-handed?"

"No, but . . . ." Her common sense returned. There was no need to explain that left-handed children didn't have to have one left-handed parent. Jacob was smart enough to know that. Besides, she'd let herself get trapped by protesting too much. If she weren't careful, Jacob would get suspicious.

Jacob was acutely aware of Rachel's turmoil. He'd baited her, and she had taken the bait. Once again he was amazed at how fiercely she fought to keep every aspect of her life a secret from him. Red flags went up and warning bells sounded. He glanced across the playground at the little boy on the see-saw. Such a sturdy, well-built little fellow, he thought, not at all like his father. Jacob remembered Bob as being so slim, he was almost skinny. He'd also been very dark, with olive skin, black eyes, black hair. As far as he could see, Benjy didn't have a single one of his father's characteristics.

"A boy needs a father to play ball with him. I suppose you'll marry again." He watched Rachel compose herself. Even in the ninety-degree heat she looked elegant, as if she should be wearing pearls and a tiara instead of shorts and halter top. One of the things he'd loved most about her was the unexpected contrast between her cool good looks and her hot explosive passions.

"I suppose."

"Will it be somebody nice and safe this time?"

"Nice and safe?"

"You know what I mean—a separate bedroom type of fellow, like Bob."

"That's none of your concern."

He was quiet a moment, gazing across the playground at Benjy and Vashti on the seesaws.

"Yes. It's my concern."

"Of all the arrogant, conceited—"

His boom of laughter stopped her. "You presume too much, Rachel. Did you think I still loved you because of the way I kissed you?" Her green eyes darkened to jade, and her face flushed. "It's not love that motivates me. I just don't relish the thought of having to follow two people around in order to find out the truth."

He stood up, enjoying the advantage of towering over her. Casually, as if the contact were unplanned, he propped one foot on the bench, brushing the toe of his jogging shoe against Rachel's thigh. She jumped as if firecrackers had been lit under her skin, then tried to cover herself by brushing at her leg.

"Ants," she said.

He lifted one eyebrow but said nothing.

"We *do* have ants down here in the summer. Everywhere."

Leaning down, he cupped her face. "Rachel . . .

Rachel. How long are you going to keep pretending with me?"

She didn't try to deny anything. "Go away, Jacob."

"I will. For now." His thumbs circled her skin, then he released her face. "But I'll be back. I promise you that."

She watched him leave. Fear clawed at her throat as he detoured by the seesaw and said good-bye to Benjy and Vashti. Both gave him big hugs. Seeing her son there, wrapped in his father's arms, made her weep inside. Strange how one lie could become a web of deception that tangled so many lives—hers, her father's, Jacob's, Benjy's, Bob's. Only Vashti remained untouched by the lie. She accepted all the stories, the premature birth, the quarrel over Jacob's life-style, the lack of other children due to Bob's poor health and her career.

Only when Jacob was out of sight did Rachel move from the bench. Then she joined her son and Vashti for a laughter-filled summer ride on the merry-go-round.

Jacob wasted no time after he left the park.

Jerking Bob's hated shirt over his head and flinging it into a corner of his motel room, he picked up the phone.

"Rick," he said without preliminaries, "is the Baron serviced and ready to fly?"

"You bet."

"How soon can you leave?"

Rick paused for a quick swig of orange soda. Jacob could hear the slosh of liquid in the bottle, almost see the way Rick tipped back in his chair, his throat working as the sweet warm drink went down. The bottle thunked against the wooden desktop.

"As soon as I make a couple of phone calls."

Jacob laughed. "Only two women? You must be slipping."

"Slow night."

"I'll meet you at the airport."

Rick McGill didn't emerge from the Baron; he bounded out like the leader of a marching band. Blond hair disheveled, brown eyes crinkled with laughter, lean body swaggering, he strode across the tarmac toward Jacob.

They clapped each other on the shoulder, their usual brotherly greeting. The same age, almost the same height, with Rick having two inches over Jacob, the same devil-may-care smiles, they might have been brothers instead of comrades. They had met the year Jacob went into fire-fighting. Rick had already been part of the team Jacob had joined. They fought fires together, drank together, caroused together. Best friends almost from the moment they had met, they kept no secrets. Rick knew that Rachel Windham Devlin had broken Jacob's heart, and Jacob knew that no woman would ever break Rick's heart. He loved them all, and he was far too cagey to let one get under his skin.

"Man, it's hotter that Maria Jaurez's kisses down here." Rick peeled off his poplin flight jacket and slung it over his shoulder.

"You would know. Let's step inside the lounge, where it's cooler."

"Reckon they'd have a warm orange soda?"

"From the glimpse I got of that waitress, she can heat up anything just by looking at it."

"I see what you mean," Rick said as they slid into a booth at the back of the small airport lounge. "She might be worth checking out."

"You may not be in Biloxi that long."

"Sounds serious, Jacob." Rick leaned back and studied his friend. "You look serious. Don't tell me you're letting Rachel get under your skin again."

"It's not Rachel." Jacob had doubts about the truth of that statement, but now was not the time for sharing confidences of that sort. "It's what she's hiding."

"What's that?"

"Damned if I know. That's why I called you down here. In spite of your flighty personality, you're the best investigator I know."

"Flighty, huh? I resemble that remark."

"You sure as hell do." They laughed together, then Jacob leaned across the small table toward his friend. "I want her investigated, Rick."

"There are better men for the job. I haven't done any serious investigation in seven years. My skills are rusty."

"You're the only man I trust for this job."

"It's done. Tell me what you want."

"I want to know every move she's made in the last six years, where she's lived, where she's worked, where she's played. And I want to know about her son. Hell, I don't even know when and where the boy was born."

Rick's brown eyes lit with interest. "Are you thinking what I think you're thinking?"

Jacob leaned back and ran a hand through his hair. "I don't know what to believe anymore. All I know is that Rachel is extraordinarily determined to get me out of her life, and I intend to find out why."

"I'll do what I can."

"Take the Mustang. It's faster than the Baron."

They ordered sandwiches, then settled back to talk. Both men had the same passionate approach to business that they had to pleasure. They were intense and serious as they talked, generating so much high-powered energy, the waitress speculated to another customer that the two men in the corner booth were secret agents on a government mission.

When Rick left, Jacob's adrenaline was still high. He felt the same readiness as when he faced a raging old field fire. But Rachel Windham Devlin was a fire of a different kind. And he would subdue it, just as he had all the others. Even if it took the rest of his life.

On the way out of the airport, he picked up the afternoon paper. The item he was looking for was in the social column. He scanned it with interest, then glanced at his watch. He still had time, he thought, time for one more surprise for Rachel.

Rachel usually loved parties of this kind, small intimate gatherings of people who had much in common—a love of music, art, theater; an interest in politics; and heightened social consciousness.

She stood on the fringes of the small group, surveying the scene with the eagle eye of a hostess with a reputation for excellence. That afternoon the decorators and caterers had transformed the first floor of her house into a veritable sea of flowers and food. Now gardenias, white roses, and white orchids bloomed from the tops of polished tables. They floated in front of the French doors, suspended by baskets on golden cord, and they festooned the bandstand that had been erected at one end of the ballroom.

The band was playing a sad song, and guests dressed in satin and sequins and in tuxes glided across the marble floor. It was a beautiful party, but Rachel wasn't enjoying it. Not tonight. Not after spending the morning in the park seeing her son play ball with his real father.

"It's fabulous, Rachel. And so are you," said Louie Vincetti, owner of the Blue Bayou, the ritzy club where she sang. As civic-minded as he was sharp in business, he'd closed the club for the weekend in order to devote time to his favorite charity.

"Thanks, Louie."

Louis looked at her with his sharp black eyes, pulled out a cigar, and stuck it, unlit, into his mouth. "Tell Uncle Louie what's bothering you, babe. A beautiful thing like you should be wearing a smile to go with those sapphires and diamonds." He patted her shoulder as he talked, his square little hand almost keeping rhythm with the band.

Coming from any other man, that kind of familiar language and attention would have offended Rachel. But it didn't coming from Louie. He was her friend, her adviser, and her surrogate father. He'd taken her under his wing when she and Bob had moved to Biloxi, and had sensed that singing was more than a talent for her, more than a job. Louie's own heart was so big, he instinctively seemed to understand the hearts of others. With Rachel, he'd always known that singing was survival to her, a way of compensating for a bland marriage, a safe way of channeling her passion.

"I guess it's too soon after Bob's death for a party

of this kind, even if the proceeds do go to your favorite charity."

"Hmmmm." Louie chomped down on the end of his cigar and gazed into space.

Rachel, knowing she hadn't told him the truth and afraid of offending him, hastened to rectify her mistake. "Not that I'm sorry I agreed to throw this party, you understand. I'm always happy to do what I can for your animals." She was referring to the Louie Vincetti Animal Adoption Home, a program Louie had set up three years ago to get stray animals off the street and into the homes of people who would love them.

Louie loved hearing the animals referred to as his. He took great pride in turning everything he touched into a success, and it pleased him that every stray animal in Biloxi was now referred to as Louie's cat or Louie's dog. Volunteers flocked to help him get the strays into his adoption home.

He turned and smiled at one of his all-time favorite people. "At two hundred dollars a head, and with twenty-five couples here, that's an easy ten thousand dollars raised for the home in one night." He shifted the cigar in his mouth and moved his hand down to pat Rachel's arm. "That's not counting the large donation I got this afternoon."

"That's wonderful, Louie. Do I know the donor?"

"Could be. He just walked through the door."

Jacob Donovan stood in the doorway, tight jeans encasing his legs, white shirt open at the throat, leather bomber jacket worn with as much panache as any movie hero Rachel had ever seen. His casual clothes were as out of place among the tuxedos and glittering ball gowns as sin at a tent revival, but he was easily the most commanding presence in the room. There was a fierce wild charm about him, as if he had found secrets in the skies that ordinary people only dared dream of, as if those mysteries were stored, shining and bright, in his soul.

He scanned the crowd. When he saw Rachel, he smiled. It was a smile that could topple kingdoms. She tasted fear and excitement in her suddenly dry mouth.

He crossed the crowded room with an ease that had always been his trademark. Everything came easy for Jacob Donovan, she thought, everything except giving up.

"Hello, Rachel. Mr. Vincetti." Although he acknowledged Louie's presence, he had eyes only for Rachel.

"Jacob." She made herself smile, forced herself to extend a cool hand. She wanted to rant and rave. She wanted to pull a pot of gardenias down on his head. "Thank you for your generous contribution. Louie told me about it."

"I'm an animal lover myself." As he spoke, he undressed Rachel with his eyes. Bit by sizzling bit, he peeled away the diamond, sapphire, and pearl clip earrings, tossed aside the matching necklace, raked her bare shoulders, then ripped away the black evening gown. Lord, he thought, she was the most stunning creature he'd ever seen. Some women got more beautiful with maturity, and she was one of them. The dress was classic and simple, strapless to show off her shoulders, the bodice tightly fitted to enhance her small breasts, and the skirt flowing to billow against her incredible legs and tease a man to distraction. Not that she needed a fancy dress to make her lovely. Her face alone was enough to make his knees weak.

He began talking, more to distract himself than

anything else. "When I read in the afternoon paper that your benefit was sold out, I contacted Mr. Vincetti. He agreed to let me come, for a price."

"Five thousand," Louie said.

"Five thousand?" The size of the contribution struck new terror into Rachel's heart. When Jacob had sworn to be her shadow, she'd expected that he would be at all her performances, had even expected he would connive his way into her home. What she hadn't known was that he was willing to pay so much to be with her. Not to be with her, she corrected herself, to find out her secret.

"He's a generous man. Too bad he missed hearing you sing." Louie pocketed his well-chewed cigar. "She's already done the benefit show, Donovan."

"That's all right. For my money, I expect a private performance."

Rachel's chin came up, and her gaze locked with his. "You'll get no private performances from me, Jacob Donovan—singing or otherwise."

He lifted one wicked eyebrow. "Singing is your only performance that interests me now."

"Damn you, Jacob Donovan."

The minute they had laid eyes on each other, no one else in the room existed for them. The old man standing at their side, avidly taking in every word and every gesture, was completely forgotten.

"Rachel, Ra-chel," Louie chided in singsong rhythm, "the boy paid a king's ransom to hear you sing. One more song." He put his arm around her shoulder and squeezed. "For me, sweetheart, then we'll call it a night."

She turned to Louie. "For you." Then she swept toward the bandstand without looking back. She knew Jacob was watching every move she made. She could feel his gaze on her.

Leaning down, she whispered to the band leader. When he had finished the dance number, he walked to the microphone. "Rachel Devlin has graciously consented to honor us with one more number—'As Time Goes By.' "

Rachel thought she could sing the entire song without looking at Jacob. But she was mistaken. The magnetic pull of his blue eyes was irresistible. One look and she was hooked, yearning for him, crooning to him, singing only for him, only for Jacob. He knew. She could tell by the satisfied look on his face. Why? her mind screamed. Why did he want to torture her? He'd said he wanted the truth, but why did he keep resurrecting the passion?

She closed her eyes, trying to shut him out as she finished her song. But he was there, imprinted on her mind. His face haunted her, taunted her, making the song so sweet-sad, a tear trickled down her cheek.

When it was over, the audience went wild with applause. They rushed the bandstand, congratulating her over and over again, praising her singing, the party, the animal shelter. Louie edged his way to her side, taking in his share of the praise.

Jacob waited patiently beside the French doors. His time would come. Soon. As soon as the crowd left. He leaned against the door frame, drowning in the presence of Rachel and the fragrance of gardenias suspended from the ceiling beside his head.

As the crowd began to leave, Louie pulled Rachel aside for a private word. "That man, Rachel—Jacob Donovan. You two have been lovers?"

"How did you know?"

"A man sees these things." He shook a cigar from his pack and clamped it between his teeth. "Something's burning a hole in his heart. Yours too. You want to tell old Louie about it, sweetheart?"

Rachel put a hand on his arm. "Thanks, Louie, but not now. Maybe sometime, but not right now." She let herself scan the crowd. Jacob was still there. She'd known he wouldn't leave.

"I've had three wives, Rachel. Loved them all in my own way. I know about love. When you need good, sound advice, you come to old Louie, huh? You come to me, sweetheart."

She kissed his cheek. "How would I get along without you?"

"Very well, my dear. Very well, indeed." Louie patted her shoulders, her arms, and her cheeks in his fatherly way, clucking and murmuring in Italian. "You come to old Louie, you hear?" With those final words, he followed the last stragglers out the door.

Rachel leaned against the piano, seeking its solid support, while the band packed to leave. The room was silent except for the rattling of cymbals, the shudder of the drums, and the snapping of locks on the instrument cases.

And then, she was alone with Jacob Donovan.

Peeling off his bomber jacket and slinging it over his shoulder, he walked toward her. She pressed against the piano.

"How did you know?" she asked.

"About tonight?"

"Yes."

"Vashti told me this morning in the park. Then I read it in the afternoon papers." He put one foot on the bandstand, propped his arm on his knee, and looked deep into her eyes. "You're a busy lady."

"I try to be."

"I admire a person who is not selfish with her talents."

"You admire me, Jacob?"

Their gazes clashed. They were playing a game, and both of them knew it.

"I admire your voice. Were you singing to me tonight, Rachel?"

"No."

"You once said you sang all your songs for me."

"That was a long time ago."

"Six years."

"Yes."

They were silent a while, their breathing a harsh sound in the room. Jacob leaned closer, his penetrating gaze making Rachel flushed and hot.

"You're wearing pearls again, Rachel."

Her hand went to the choker of twisted pearls and diamonds, brushed over the three large sapphires set in the center.

"Not just pearls."

"But pearls, nonetheless."

She thought she would drown in his blue eyes as memories washed over her. Pearls. She remembered so well. . . .

It had been seven years ago. Jacob had bought her a single strand of perfect pearls for her birthday. Standing in the bedroom of her apartment in Greenville, he'd lifted her hair, fastening them on her neck.

"Pearls become you, Rachel. You should always wear them."

She turned in his arms and gave him a long, leisurely kiss. "For you, I'll always wear pearls."

He laughed. "One kiss always makes me hungry."

"For food?" she teased.

"For more." He bent her over backward, nuzzling her neck, nudging the top button on her cashmere sweater.

"Jacob . . . Jacob. . . ." One touch from him, and she was liquid with need.

In answer to her pleas, he unbuttoned her sweater and cast it aside. Still without speaking, his eyes burning into hers, he unfastened her skirt and let it drift to the floor. Her satin slip whispered as he slipped it over her head. His fingertips dragged slowly over her skin, sending shivers through her body. Hooking his thumbs in the waistband of her panties, he slid them down her legs.

When she was wearing only pearls and high heels, he took her. Fast and hard. There on her brass bed with the moonlight filtering through the curtains. . . .

She still remembered how the pearls had felt against her skin, warm and alive. Sensual.

She shook her head and raked her hands through her heavy hair.

"The past is always with us, isn't it, Rachel?"

"Damn you for knowing, Jacob."

Laughing, he reached for her hand. "Come."

She tried to jerk her hand away, but he kept it in a tight grip. "I'm not going anywhere with you, Jacob. Who do you think you are to come barging into my house, ordering me around?"

"I'm the man you once loved." His face tightened. "And I don't intend to spend the rest of the evening standing here arguing with you."

He swept her off her feet and tossed her casually over his shoulder.

"Put me down, you pirate."

He swatted her fanny and continued his march to the door. "Behave."

"Just where do you think you're taking me?"

"Down memory lane."

The French doors clicked shut behind him, and he began to whistle "Waltzing Matilda."

Five

The plane stood on a deserted private runway ten miles east of Biloxi. It was Jacob's twin-engine Baron, and the private strip belonged to Captain Mark Waynesburg. When Jacob had called that afternoon, he'd been happy to allow another fly-boy to use it.

Jacob parked the rental car, opened the door, and lifted Rachel out. Slinging her over his shoulder again, he walked toward the plane.

"Put me down. I can walk."

"I'm not taking any chances."

"Look, I've given in to this kidnapping graciously—"

"Graciously! You call all that ranting and raving gracious?" He patted her bottom and kept on walking.

"I never rant and rave. I merely express my opinions."

"The way you express your opinions is enough to make the United Nations sit up and take notice."

"You used to call it spirit. You used to love it."

He still did, but he wasn't about to tell her. Things were already bad enough for him, with Rachel's body pressed against him front and back and her fragrance making him rigid with desire. The sooner he got her off his shoulder, the better.

When they were beside the plane, he lowered her to the ground, but he kept his arm around her waist, holding her close against his chest. The wind caught her hair and blew it back into his face. The soft scent of roses nearly drove him wild.

"Rachel." Her name was a sigh on his lips.

She looked up at him with eyes filled with passion. From the moment he'd walked into her ballroom, she'd known they were fated to come together. Heated by the love song she'd sung to him, spurred by the flame in his eyes, melting from the contact of being flung over his shoulder, she laced her arms around his neck.

"Love me, Jacob."

His expression was fierce, then his lips slammed down on hers. She opened for him, welcoming his tongue. He caught her hips and dragged her closer. Through his jeans, through the heavy satin of her skirt, she felt the heat of him, the size of him.

"Jacob, Jacob," she murmured.

"Ahhh, Rachel. . . ." His mouth seared her skin. "I can't resist."

"Don't try." Her head dropped back on her limp neck as he aimed his kisses lower. His tongue found the hollow where her breasts pushed up above the top of her strapless gown. The heat consumed her.

She caught his shoulders, digging her fingers into the soft leather of his bomber jacket. She wanted him. She was moist and hot, bursting with the need to feel him, to *know* him once again.

He kissed every inch of her exposed skin, nudging and tasting and probing and licking until even the pearls and diamonds at her throat burned her. When he took possession of her mouth, she moaned and leaned into him, sucking hungrily at his lips.

"Rachel. . . ." He tried to pull away, then found himself drawn back to the mindless madness of her kiss. She was a sorceress, a beautiful alchemist who was changing him, turning him from his purpose.

With a muttered curse, he put his hand on her shoulders and roughly pushed her away.

"It's the heat," he said, "the damned Biloxi heat."

They both knew better. It was not the heat of the night that had them under a spell: It was the heat of passion.

Rachel saw her advantage and took it.

"You were never a coward, Jacob," she taunted.

"I was never a fool either." He got up, then pulled Rachel up beside him. He jerked off his bomber jacket and slung it around her shoulders. "Here. Wear this. You'll get cold."

"In this heat?"

"We won't be in this heat much longer. We'll be there." He swept his arm wide to encompass the starlit sky.

The shock of his statement was enough to cool her ardor. "Are you mad?"

"Yes." His smile was rueful. "Totally without reason. Certifiably insane." He opened the door to the cockpit. "You'd do well not to argue with me while I'm in this condition."

She balked. "I'm not getting in that airplane."

"Yes, you are."

"No! I hate to fly. You know that."

"Tonight you'll show me exactly how much you hate the sky. You'll explain to me precisely why."

Rachel glimpsed the personal demons that drove him. The plane rose up beside them, gleaming in the moonlight, a ghostly machine, a diabolical machine that had haunted her since her mother's death. Her chin went up. She wouldn't be defeated, not this time.

"I'll show you, Jacob. Help me into this damned machine, and I'll tell you exactly why I hate it." She put her arms into the sleeves of his jacket, then turned to face him. "And after tonight, I will never fly again."

He helped her into the cockpit, leaning over her to strap her in. Her face was pale. He touched his hand to her cheek, already regretting his tactics.

"Don't be afraid, Rachel. I won't let any harm come to you."

"I'm not afraid." She pulled the jacket close around her throat, covering her glittering necklace.

Jacob's hands played gently over her face. "I want you to understand, this is one problem that should have been resolved between us long ago."

"You never tried to understand my viewpoint, Jacob."

"Lord knows, I tried to, but I suppose you're right. I could never understand how anyone could hate and fear something so beautiful." He gazed into her eyes, willing her to understand—and to forgive. Then he turned resolutely and fastened on his headset. "Tonight you will see that flying is almost a religious experience. In the sky, in that vast and mysterious cathedral—" he paused, his arm swinging upward toward the stars "—you will feel almost as if you could touch the face of God."

They were silent as Jacob concentrated on getting the Baron aloft. He taxied the craft smoothly down the runway, gaining speed, pulling back on the throttle, lifting the nose, climbing, climbing into the stars.

A sense of exhilaration filled him until he almost shouted with joy. In the sky, he was both servant and commander. In the vastness of the heavens, he was as small and insignificant as a grain of sand. And yet . . . he was master. He commanded the machine that carried him. Like a well-trained dog, the plane obeyed his slightest order. In the Baron he could transcend the earth, traverse the heavens. All the wonder and mystery of the sky was his.

They climbed higher, higher than eagles.

Huddled into the copilot's seat, Rachel forgot her fear when she saw his face. The only time she'd ever seen a face glow like his was more than five years before, when Benjamin had been born. Holding her newborn son in her arms, she'd seen herself in the mirror.

She looked out the window, trying to see her surroundings with Jacob's eyes. But all she saw was darkness, interrupted here and there with a sprinkling of stars.

The Baron lifted into the sky. At 7,500 feet, Jacob turned to Rachel.

"Button your jacket. The temperature is zero degrees up here." He flipped a switch that regulated the plane's heater.

Even in the enclosed plane, she noticed the chill. Nodding, she obeyed Jacob, then she turned from him to look out the window. She was beginning to relax. She didn't know if it had to do with Jacob's presence or her own rationalization that she was too old to let her fear of flying continue to dominate her life. It was only part of the reason she'd left Jacob, but it was the sole reason she had never accepted singing engagements overseas. Bob had known that and had not tried to change her mind. If possible, he'd always booked her engagements so that they'd have plenty of time to drive. Several times she'd had to make quick trips to New York or Los Angeles and had forced herself to fly, but she'd never conquered the fear.

She glanced at the man beside her. Things would have been different if she had married Jacob. She knew that now. He would never have passively accepted her fear of flying. At some point he would have done exactly what he was doing now—kidnapped her and taken her into the air to let her experience the adventure through his eyes.

She hugged his coat around her and smiled. Being with a swashbuckling man certainly had its appeal.

"Rachel." She jumped when he spoke her name. He smiled at her. "You're not scared, are you?"

"No. I don't love it, mind you, but I have confidence in the pilot."

"Good. We're going into that cloud bank just above us. You won't see anything outside the window until we climb out at about fourteen thousand feet. Think of it as taking a stroll through heavy fog."

If he hadn't explained what was happening, she might have been scared. Instead she felt only a slight tremor as the Baron cut through the bottom of the clouds and entered the darkness that was without stars. Puffs of dark gray clouds rolled by the windows like dirty snow that had banked along some cold street corner. Smoky wisps floated toward them, then rose up toward the dark columns of clouds that surrounded the plane.

"Are you okay, Rachel?"

"Yes."

"We're almost there."

Suddenly the nose of the plane lifted out of the

clouds. Color so brilliant it dazzled her eyes poured into the plane. The cockpit was filled with a golden glow. It shone on her skin, glinted off the diamonds at her throat and ears.

"Jacob!"

"It's the moon, Rachel. Look."

The moon, full and bright and so close she could almost touch it, hung between two banks of clouds, darkness above and darkness below. Its shining splendor touched the tops of the cloud mountains, gilding them.

"It's beautiful," she said.

"Have you ever seen anything like it?"

"No."

"And you never will. Except up here in the sky." He watched her, watched her awe-struck expression. "This is one of the reasons I fly, Rachel. This is one of the reasons I will never give it up."

"Nor should you." She turned to face him. "It's like being in the middle of a lovely song, Jacob. It's like seeing the most incredible love song ever written come to life."

He smiled. "You understand."

At last, she did. "Yes."

Too late for regrets, he thought. Too late to wish he'd brought her with him into the sky more than six years ago.

"Then let's go home," he said.

In silence they left the ethereal otherworld of the sky and descended once more to the earth. So smooth was the landing that there was no indication they weren't still flying except for the hiss of the tires as they connected with the runway.

They sat for two full minutes, unwilling to break the spell that bound them together. At last Jacob spoke.

"Is this why, Rachel?"

She knew what he meant. "Partially, Jacob. I could see only the danger not the beauty. I'm sorry."

"So am I."

He helped her from the cockpit, careful not to keep her hand too long lest even that brief contact undo his control. Inside the car, she peeled off his jacket and handed it back to him. The scent of roses clung to the garment. He flung the jacket carelessly onto the back seat, as if he hadn't noticed, but he knew it would be a long, long time before he could wear that jacket without thinking of Rachel. Maybe he never could.

Neither spoke as they drove back to her house. Rachel was grateful he didn't question her, thankful he didn't press for the truth. She had other things on her mind. Jacob. She had Jacob on her mind.

He let her out at the gate, allowing her to make a graceful exit. If he had insisted on coming inside, insisted on kissing her, she didn't know what the consequences would have been. As she watched him drive away, she knew she had to leave. One by one Jacob was crumbling her defenses. If she stayed in Biloxi, she knew that her heart would betray her. It belonged to Jacob, always had, always would. She knew that now. The tragedy was that she couldn't listen to her heart. She had to think of Benjamin.

She didn't bother trying to sleep. In the few hours of night that were left, she changed into slacks and packed her bags. When the first light of morning glowed on the eastern horizon, she tiptoed into Benjamin's room and packed for him too. As she packed, she could hear Vashti stirring. Rachel smiled. Vashti had never been one to while away the day in bed.

She went into the kitchen, stopping by the stove

long enough to pour herself a cup of coffee. It was strong and black, perked the old-fashioned way in an aluminum pot over a gas flame.

Vashti watched her for a while before she spoke her piece.

"You look like you haven't slept a wink."

"I haven't. I had to pack." She took another fortifying sip of coffee. "Benjamin and I are leaving Biloxi today."

"Just like that." Vashti snapped her fingers. "You're going to tuck tail and run, just because Jacob Donovan has come to town."

"How did you know?"

"Seeing the two of you together, it wouldn't take an army intelligence officer to figure it out. It's a mistake. That's what it is." Vashti banged the lid on the flour cannister for emphasis.

"It's self-preservation. Jacob and I couldn't make it together six years ago, and we can't make it together now—not that he'd want to try."

"Ha!"

"Besides, I need a vacation. *You* need a vacation." She left her coffee at the table and went to cajole the older woman. "Where do you want to go? Just name the place, and we'll go there. How about Florida? We'll drive down to Orlando and take Benjy to Disney World. Or Mexico? Would you rather go to Mexico?"

"I'd rather sit right here in Biloxi and watch Jacob sweep you off your feet and down to the altar, where you should have gone with him six years ago. That's what I'd rather do." She slung flour onto the dough board and pounded her biscuits with a vengeance. " 'Course, some folks I know can't seem to see the forest for the trees. Always got to be running scared.

Always got to be dragging this old woman around somewhere folks don't know how to speak proper English. All that foreign jibberish. Can't anybody talk the King's English except Mississippians. It's enough to make a body want to retire."

Rachel let her grumble. It was Vashti's way. She'd protest long and loud, air her opinions four times each, until there was positively no room for doubt about how she felt. But she'd go. She loved Benjamin and Rachel too much to stay behind. Rachel was counting on that.

Vashti turned from the dough board. "How soon do we leave?"

"As soon as I can call Louie and tell him."

Thirty minutes later Rachel had her boss on the phone.

"It's sudden, sweetheart. But I agree. A vacation will do you good."

"I know it's short notice, Louie, but under the circumstances, there's nothing else I can do."

"Take all the time you need, sweetheart. I'll get the Crawdads to come in next week and fill your spot. They've been pestering me for months to give them a try." He chuckled. "The Blue Bayou is considered the launching pad to success."

"Thanks, Louie."

"Anytime, sweetheart. Say, you didn't mention where you'd be going."

"Somewhere as far away from here as I can get."

"Take my advice. Head north where the sun won't fry your brains every time you step out the door. I got relatives in Jersey who'd be glad to see you."

"And I'd be glad to see them. But there's a favorite

little spot of mine on Lake George in Florida, close enough to Orlando to take Benjy to Disney World but far enough from civilization to be a real retreat. Maybe next time, Louie."

The three of them were on the road by nine o'clock, Rachel driving, Vashti buckled in beside her, and Benjy bouncing against his seatbelt in the back, pretending the BMW was an airplane and he was the pilot. With the little boy providing the sound effects, they zoomed east on Highway 90, skirting along the edge of the gulf, heading to Florida.

They took their first bathroom break at Pascagoula, less than fifty miles out of Biloxi. As usual, when Benjy was one of the travelers, the pit stop became a real adventure.

"I bet they got a real gum ball machine," he told his mother, tugging her toward the small service station.

She smiled. "I'll bet they do. Why don't we go inside and find out? Are you coming, Vashti?"

Vashti heaved herself out of the front seat. "You two go on. It'll take me fifteen minutes in the powder room. When you've got a body sculpted by Sara Lee, these things take longer."

Clutching her straw purse and holding onto her straw hat so the gulf breezes wouldn't blow it off her head, she watched the two of them go. She never traveled without her hat, for she didn't believe in letting the sun ruin her complexion. She also didn't believe in raising children without a father.

Her straw sandals slapped against the concrete as she lumbered her way around the service station to the pay telephone. Fishing a quarter out of her purse, she wedged herself into the phone booth and picked up the receiver. She hoped the Lord would forgive her for meddling. But under the circumstances, she didn't see what else she could do.

The phone rang six times before she heard the click at the other end. She smiled. Everything was going to work out all right.

"This is Vashti," she said. Then, while Rachel and Benjy were putting pennies into the gum ball machine, she began to tell her story—at least part of it.

Jacob was in Florida long before Rachel arrived. He'd flown the Baron into Daytona Beach and had rented a jeep for the drive inland to Lake George. Vashti had been very specific about the cabin Rachel always rented. Jacob had the good fortune to rent the one next door to hers. A copse of trees separated the cabins, but sitting on his front porch looking through his binoculars, he had a good view of Rachel's retreat. Only a few low-hanging tree branches kept his view from being perfect.

He had learned patience when he first became a fire fighter. The raging conflagrations in oil fields didn't respond to anything else. There were no quick fixes for out-of-control fires. Nothing paid off except skill and finesse and weeks of steady, dogged battling. It would be the same with Rachel, he thought. He wouldn't give up, and she would finally crack. She'd tell him the truth, then he could put her out of his life.

That last thought gave him no joy. He took a long swig of cool lemonade and tried to figure out why. But a mosquito was buzzing his ears and sweat was trickling down his chest, and it was too damned hot for introspection. He gave it up and padded inside barefoot to get a magazine. *Aviation Today.* He'd read while he waited.

The sound of a car brought his head up. Training his binoculars through the trees, he saw Rachel. She looked tired. He must be getting to her. Instead of feeling triumphant, he felt a gentle wave of compassion wash over him. He wanted to run through the trees and take her in his arms. He wanted to smooth her tumbled hair back from her face and croon soothing words to her. His hands tightened on the binoculars. He couldn't afford to get soft. Not with Rachel. He wasn't looking to have his heart broken again.

Jacob smiled when Benjy came into view. That boy sure wasn't tired. He raced up and down the porch steps, taking his vacation gear into the cabin one piece at a time—first the little overnight bag, then the beach ball, then a mesh sack of toy planes, then his baseball glove, and finally the bat.

"I wish Mr. Donoben was here to play ball." His clear little boy's voice echoed through the trees. Jacob smiled. He remembered how it was to be a boy. There'd been no such thing as talking in a normal tone. Everything had to be yelled so the busy grown-ups would be sure to hear.

Rachel bent over her son and said something. Jacob could only guess what she was saying. There was nothing shrill about her voice. It was silk and velvet, all soft melodies that cut right through to a man's soul. He closed his eyes, remembering how it was to hear that musical voice whispering love words in his ear.

Fool, he chided himself. His eyes snapped open, and he looked across the way. Rachel was alone on her porch, standing very still. She was watching him, and for a moment he thought she knew. That was impossible, of course. The cabins were too far apart. She'd be able to see the figure of a man. That was all. Without binoculars, there was no way she could know his identity.

Jacob tipped back his glass and let the cool lemonade wash down his throat. It was hot in Florida.

Rachel stood on the porch a moment, watching. Her heart did a crazy rhythm, and for an instant she thought the man she saw sitting on the front porch next door was Jacob. It was crazy, of course. He'd still be in Biloxi, probably just now discovering she was no longer there.

A line of sweat trickled from under her heavy hair and inched down her cheek. She pushed at the hair with her right hand, lifting it off her neck to try and catch a cool breeze from the lake. She was so hot! It was the weather, of course. It was sweltering in Florida.

Dragging her gaze away from the man next door, she went inside to join Vashti and Benjy.

Six

The sound of a harmonica woke Rachel. At first she didn't know what had brought her out of her restless sleep, then she heard the faint strains of the mouth harp, plaintive and sweet, floating through her screened windows like night-crazed moths. She sat up, her cotton gown bunched around her thighs and her hair tangled and damp. The music drifted on the hot air. "Waltzing Matilda."

Her breath caught high in her throat, and her hands flew to her lips. Jacob couldn't be in Florida. And yet the song was his trademark, the only one he knew. She remembered so well the day he'd learned it. . . .

They'd been on a picnic beside the Mississippi River. She'd just come home from a singing engagement in New Orleans, and they were celebrating.

"I brought you a gift, Jacob." She held a small

package out to him and watched his eyes light up. Jacob was like a little boy. He loved presents.

Smiling, he took the package. "You thought of me while you were gone, then?"

"Every minute of every day."

"What about the nights?"

"The nights too. Every song I sang was for you. Every dream I dreamed was of you."

He cupped her face and kissed her, quick and hard. "I missed you too." Releasing her, he leaned back against the trunk of a weeping willow tree and tore open the package. His smile changed to a chuckle. The small blues harp lay in his hand, glinting in the sun. "Does it come with lessons?"

"Private lessons."

He kissed her again, longer, with more passion this time.

"Hmmmm, sounds good to me. When do we start?" He reached for the top button of her blouse.

She swatted his hand away. "*Music* lessons, Jacob. If you're going to be my husband, then it's high time for you to learn a little bit about music. The harmonica is a perfect instrument for you. All it takes is a little concentration. It will be just like whistling . . . or humming."

"I do both of those off key."

"I know. . . ."

She'd given him his first harmonica lesson there by the river. "Waltzing Matilda" was the only song he knew, and the only song he ever tried to learn. He'd said one all-occasion song was enough for him. He'd learned the whole thing that afternoon.

As Rachel sat in her bed, listening to the song

drift through the window, she listened for the one note. It came to her clearly through the night, third bar, first beat. Jacob always missed the B-flat.

She pushed aside the tangled sheet and reached for her robe. The thin cotton felt cool against her overheated skin. Her slippers made soft slapping sounds on the wooden floor as she padded through the cabin to her front porch. Leaning on the railing, she peered through the night.

There was a full moon riding on the top branches of the trees. The silvery light illuminated the waters of Lake George, gilded the swaying pines and high- lighted the hair of the man sitting on his front porch—bright red hair, wild and unruly.

The false note sang through the night once more as Jacob Donovan played the only song he knew.

Rachel acted on instinct. Without even changing into walking shoes, she hurried down her front porch steps and through the small grove of trees. When she was close enough to see him clearly, she stopped. Rustlings in the leaves at her feet made her jump. She'd been foolish to come. What insanity had pro- pelled her through the night? What impossible dreams had sent her flying to Jacob's side?

Drawing her thin robe around her shoulders, she turned to go.

"Rachel." He spoke her name quietly but with great command. "Don't go."

She hesitated, torn between common sense and foolish passion. The passion won.

"Jacob." His name was soft on her lips as she glided through the darkness toward him. When she was at his front steps, she stopped, leaning against the rough wooden railing. "I heard your song."

"You weren't sleeping well?"

"No."

"I couldn't sleep either . . . the heat."

"Yes. It must be the heat."

His compelling blue eyes drew her on. She couldn't bring herself to look away from them. She trembled as she climbed the steps. Even the small night breeze felt like sandpaper fingers raking over her sensitized skin. When she was on the front porch, standing only a few feet away from his tipped-back chair, she stopped.

Jacob slowly pocketed the harmonica and just as slowly lowered the front legs of his chair. His gaze never left her face.

"You shouldn't have come out in the dark by your-self, Rachel."

"I know."

"The dark can be dangerous."

Leaning down so that her hair brushed against his cheek, she looked into his eyes.

"I think the only danger is from you."

He said nothing, merely gazed at her with those hypnotic blue eyes.

"Why are you here, Jacob?"

"I thought a little night music would help me sleep."

"You know what I mean."

He reached for her hand. Giving her a lazy smile, he placed her hand on his bare chest. The crisp hairs there curled possessively around her fingers. Instinctively she dug her long nails into his flesh.

Sweat trickled down the side of her cheek, rolled between her breasts. Jacob reached toward the damp cotton gown with his free hand, lightly touching her hardened nipple.

"Ahhh, Rachel. You shouldn't have come tonight."

"I know."

His fingers circled slowly on the damp fabric. She moved closer, stepping between his blue-jeaned thighs. Far out over the lake, an osprey rose from its nest, sending its call of alarm over the moonlit waters.

"Even the birds are disturbed tonight." Jacob's voice caressed her, just as his fingers did.

She tipped her head back, baring her throat. She felt limp, almost melancholy. The heat of the night pulsed around her, and the heat of Jacob burned through her.

"Even the birds," she said as her hand reached out and tangled in his bright hair.

Jacob stood up and drew her into his arms. His movements were languid, as if time had stopped just for them.

"A Victorian gown." His smile was slow and easy. Her breath came in short, harsh spurts as he dragged his hands down her back, pressing through the fabric so that he could feel the heat of her skin. "You're a paradox, Rachel. A hoyden in cool pearls. A hot-blooded minx in a white Victorian gown." He lowered his head until their lips were a mere hair's breadth apart. "You still drive me wild."

Almost mindless now with need, she drew his head down. His lips were hungry and demanding. He pulled her hard against his hips, holding her so tightly, she could barely breathe as his mouth branded hers. They swayed together, the passion and the betrayal boiling between them and through them and around them. The kiss became a punishing contest for control, a contest neither of them could win.

They kissed until Rachel's lips felt bruised. When he lifted his head, every nerve ending in her body was crying out for more. She reached for him, caught his shoulders, and held him.

"There was never another woman who could kiss the way you do, Rachel."

"I'm glad."

"You would be."

They faced each other on the night-dark porch.

"All these years . . ." Jacob paused, his gaze locked with hers, his voice so low, she had to lean in to hear it. "All these years," he continued, "there's never been a woman who could replace you. Never a woman who could take your place in my bed."

"It was the same with me."

"Bob?"

"Bob was never you."

The osprey cried out again, his plaintive whistle sounding over the water. Jacob's face grew fierce. Suddenly he kicked the chair, sending it crashing to the porch, and swept Rachel into his arms. She pressed her lips against his neck as he carried her through the screen door. His pulse beat was fast and heavy against her lips. It matched the racing rhythm of her own heart.

The bed was small and narrow, a functional cot suitable for one. A lone mosquito buzzed outside the window, its high-pitched whine carrying through the screen. Jacob's shirt was thrown carelessly across the room's one chair, and a small brass lamp on a rickety table cast a feeble light over the bed.

Jacob braced one knee on the mattress and lowered Rachel to the white sheets. Her hair fanned out across the pillow, catching the lamplight. Jacob straddled her, his knees on either side of her hips, his hands holding her wrists above her head.

"I used to dream of having you under me like this."

"It's no dream. I'm here."

His grin tightened. "Why?"

She moved her head restlessly on the pillow. "Don't talk, Jacob," she whispered.

Still holding her hands above her head, he lowered himself to her, pressed his hips tightly into hers, pinning her to the bed. She arched to meet him.

"Do you want me?" he asked.

"Yes."

"Show me how much."

This was a Jacob she'd never known. Always with them, the loving had been a joining by mutual consent. Sometimes slow and gentle, sometimes fast and hard, their lovemaking had always been an occasion of great joy. There had never been this steel-edged dueling match. The bed had never been a battleground as it was now.

Rachel understood why and accepted it. For reasons only she knew, Jacob could never be hers. Except for this one night. Tonight she'd take what she had been longing for these past six years. In the morning she'd probably regret it, but it was a mistake she could live with.

She lifted her head off the pillow and raked her tongue across his nipples. She felt the tension in him, felt the quiver that went through his body.

"Release me and I'll show you."

All the demons of hell burned in his eyes. Without letting go, he crushed his mouth down on hers. She met the fury of his kiss with wild abandon. She writhed under him, reveling in every hard ridge and muscle, glorying in the heat that penetrated the cotton layers of her gown and robe.

She felt his kiss change. His punishing lips subtly became softer, with more passion and less anger. Groaning, he seared his mouth down the side of her neck. He nudged aside her robe and closed his mouth over her breast. His tongue wet the fabric around her nipple, circling slowly until she was peaked and hardened. She cried out in her agony of need. He took the breast deep into his mouth, his tongue laving it until she was moaning for release.

"Yes . . . Jacob . . . please . . . take . . . me."

His knee bunched her gown up between her thighs. Releasing her hands, he caught her around the waist and lifted her hips. His mouth was hot on her. The lamplight flickered over them and the room swam out of control.

"You . . . taste . . . of . . . honey . . . my Rachel."

She moved with him, straining toward his touch. Time went into slow motion, spiraling down until it stopped. Desire filled the night until there was room for nothing else, not even the pettish whine of the mosquito.

"Jacob." Her voice was a broken plea, a cry of need and passion that shattered the silence.

His control snapped. The past didn't matter; the truth could wait. At that moment, on that narrow cot in a primitive Florida cabin, he had to have Rachel. Nothing else mattered to Jacob.

Seeing his face in the dim light, Rachel *knew*. She reached for his zipper; he pulled at her gown. They were sweating and panting, frenzied as only two people too-long denied can be. His jeans thudded to the floor; the delicate fabric of her gown ripped.

And then they were joined—Jacob and his Rachel.

Six years of agonized longing were swept aside in the thunderous storm of their passion. There were no words between them, for desire such as theirs needed none. Together they took the long journey in the hot night, a journey that carried them back through time, to sweet days beside a cool river, to sultry nights under the burning stars. She knew his secrets, and he knew her pleasures. Time and time again they found ecstasy.

When it was over, when they lay pressed together, their sweaty bodies gleaming in the lamplight, Rachel lifted herself on her elbow and looked down at him. Her damp hair brushed against his face.

"This doesn't change anything," she said.

"No."

His ready agreement hurt. She knew it shouldn't have, but it did. Catching her lower lip between her teeth, she leaned over him to get her gown. He caught her shoulders and pulled her across his chest.

"Rachel . . ." The words died in his throat. Looking at her there on his narrow bed, her face suffused with the afterglow of sex, her eyes soft and deep, he couldn't remember what he'd thought to say. Not that it mattered, he told himself. They'd said it all. Nothing was changed between them.

He cupped her face gently between his hands and brought her lips to his. They were moist and slightly salty. It could have been sweat, but Jacob knew it was tears. As he kissed her, he could feel the tiny trail of tears that wet her cheeks. They sliced through his heart with the deadly accuracy of a knife.

He held her a moment longer, letting the tenderness of his kiss say, "I'm sorry, sorry for the past, sorry for the present, sorry for the future that could never be." At last, he lifted his head.

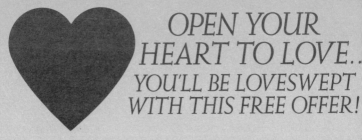

OPEN YOUR HEART TO LOVE... YOU'LL BE LOVESWEPT WITH THIS FREE OFFER!

HERE'S WHAT YOU GET:

1. **FREE! SIX NEW LOVESWEPT NOVELS!** You get 6 beautiful stories filled with passion, romance, laughter, and tears...exciting romances to stir the excitement of falling in love... again and again.

2. **FREE! A BEAUTIFUL MAKEUP CASE WITH A MIRROR THAT LIGHTS UP!** What could be more useful than a makeup case with a mirror that lights up*? Once you open the tortoise-shell finish case, you have a choice of brushes...for your lips, your eyes, and your blushing cheeks.

*(batteries not included)

3. **SAVE! MONEY-SAVING HOME DELIVERY!** Join the Loveswept at-home reader service and we'll send you 6 new novels each month. You always get 15 days to preview them before you decide. Each book is yours for only $2.09 — a savings of 41¢ per book.

4. **BEAT THE CROWDS!** You'll always receive your Loveswept books before they are available in bookstores. You'll be the first to thrill to these exciting new stories.

BE LOVESWEPT TODAY — JUST COMPLETE, DETACH AND MAIL YOUR FREE-OFFER CARD.

(DETACH AND MAIL CARD TODAY)

FREE – LIGHTED MAKEUP CASE!
FREE – 6 LOVESWEPT NOVELS!

- NO OBLIGATION
- NO PURCHASE NECESSARY

GET READY TO BE LOVESWEPT!

YES! Please send my six Loveswept novels FREE, along with my free lighted makeup case as explained on the opposite page.

NAME _____

ADDRESS_____ APT._____

CITY_____

STATE_____ ZIP_____

PLACE HEART STICKER HERE

10355

MY "NO RISK" GUARANTEE:

There's no obligation to buy — the free gifts are mine to keep. I may preview each subsequent shipment for 15 days. If I don't want it, I simply return the books within 15 days and owe nothing. If I keep them I will pay just $12.50 (I save $2.50 off the retail price for 6 books) plus postage and handling and any applicable sales tax.

Prices subject to change. Orders subject to approval.

BRo

REMEMBER!

- The free books and gift are mine to keep!
- There is no obligation!
- I may preview each shipment for 15 days!
- I can cancel anytime!

(DETACH AND MAIL CARD TODAY)

NO POSTAGE
NECESSARY
IF MAILED
IN THE
UNITED STATES

BUSINESS REPLY MAIL
FIRST-CLASS MAIL   PERMIT NO. 2456   HICKSVILLE, N.Y.

POSTAGE WILL BE PAID BY ADDRESSEE

Loveswept

Bantam Books
P.O. Box 985
Hicksville, NY 11802-9827

"Rachel—"

"Shhhh." She put her finger on his lips. "Don't say anything to spoil it." Quietly she rose from the bed. The dim glow of the lamp fell softly on her body, shading her with a mysterious, golden allure. Looking at her, Jacob's throat ached.

She pulled the gown over her head. The small jagged tear bared one breast. As she turned to get her robe, Jacob had to clench his fist to keep from reaching out to touch her.

When she covered herself with her robe, she turned to him. "I'm leaving now."

"I'll walk you home."

"No."

He caught her elbow with one hand and reached for his pants with the other.

"That's the way it's going to be, Rachel."

There was no use in arguing. She knew this mood of his. Quietly she waited for him to put on his pants and sneakers; then she allowed herself to be escorted back through the dark woods to her cabin. He didn't touch her except for his hand guiding her elbow. She was glad, for leaving Jacob was hard, and pulling out of another embrace would have been almost impossible.

At her porch steps he caught her hand. She turned to look at him, and for a moment she thought he was going to speak. But he said nothing, merely looking at her with his impossibly blue eyes.

She reached out and touched his cheek, softly, like a summer puff of dandelion. Then she went into her dark cabin. She walked straight to her cot, never looking back. She lay there rigid, her hands over her ears to shut out the sounds of Jacob's footsteps. Tears streamed down her cheeks, ran down her throat, and wet the torn neck of her gown. She had never intended to let Jacob Donovan break her heart twice. Once in a lifetime was enough.

She uncovered her ears, got off her cot, and pulled off her robe. Time to start acting sensible. Before the loving tonight, she'd known this was the way it would be. And she'd told herself she could live with the consequences. As she lay back down and pressed her face into the pillow, she prayed that she hadn't lied to herself.

Jacob didn't bother trying to sleep when he got back to his cabin. He was accustomed to sleepless nights. All fire fighters were. The only thing different about this one was that he couldn't say to himself, "It will all be over soon." After tonight, he knew that it would never be over between him and Rachel. No matter how far he traveled, no matter what truth he learned, no matter how many denials he made, he would never be free of Rachel.

He pulled a cold beer out of the small refrigerator and tipped back in a cane-bottomed chair. He had to figure out what to do next.

Jacob hadn't believed he would fall asleep, but when the tapping came on his front door, he knew he'd managed it somehow. He jerked his head off the table, flexing his stiff neck and rubbing his gritty eyes. His elbow sent the half-empty beer can clattering to the floor.

"Mr. Donoben, Mr. DonoBEN!"

"Benjy." During the night, his cramped legs had gone to sleep. He stood up, groping for the back of his chair to keep from falling. "Benjy? Is that you?"

The small boy banged into the room, freckles

scrubbed and as shiny as new pennies and a grin as big as Arkansas on his face. "Me and Vashti was looking for alligators, and she said I should come and get you but that it was a enormous big secret and we should keep quiet as lice about it. I like secrets. What's lice?"

Jacob suddenly felt awake and alive. In the presence of Rachel's child, he could push all his problems aside and simply concentrate on the joy of living. The feeling was coming back to his legs now, so he walked across the room and took the small boy's hand. It felt good in his.

"I think Vashti meant 'mice.' Where is she now?"

"Standin' on the porch being a secret."

Jacob roared with laughter.

"Come on in here, you old conspirator."

Vashti billowed in, dressed in a green muumuu, as large and spreading as an oak tree. Her self-satisfied smile stretched her painted lips so far back, it showed her gold-capped molars. Her skirts swishing and murmuring around her, she crossed the room and hugged Jacob.

"I spotted you yesterday when we unloaded, but I didn't let on."

Jacob didn't either. There were more secrets in this room than even Vashti knew about. He knew Rachel would never tell about their midnight meeting, and neither would he.

"Where's Rachel?"

"Still asleep."

"Good."

Vashti looked at him sharply, then she settled onto another of his straight-back chairs.

"We were planning to go to Disney World today,

but it seems that Rachel is tuckered out. Probably from all that driving."

"Probably," he agreed.

Vashti gave him another piercing look. "I guess we'll go tomorrow. Any other ideas?"

"Have you ever been in an airboat, Vashti?"

"No. And if the good Lord is willing, I never will. I've seen the things on 'Wild Kingdom.' Nothing but a plain out maniac would ride in one of the things."

"Can I ride in the airboat, Mr. Donoben?"

"Call me Jacob, son, and you certainly can. That is, if Vashti and your mother will approve."

Vashti smoothed her muumuu over her ample chest. "I'm in charge here. Whenever Rachel is not around, my word is law."

Jacob grinned. "And sometimes when she is around."

"Most times." Vashti leaned her elbow on the table and squinted at him. "Can you give me your personal guarantee that that airboat is safe for Benjy."

"As safe as the front pew in a church. My personal guarantee."

She leaned back, smiling. "Then I see no need to deprive this boy of your company any longer. Why don't the two of you go on and have some fun. I'll take care of Rachel."

"Oh, boy." Benjy jumped up and down in excitement. "Can we go now?"

"As soon as I can get dressed and rent the boat."

"I'll wait on the doorstep. Hurry, Mr. Dono . . . Jacob."

The door slammed behind Benjy, and Jacob took Vashti's hand. "Did I thank you for calling me, Vashti?"

"You did, but there's nothing like hearing it in

person." She patted his face. "Especially from my favorite handsome, charming Irishman."

"Thanks, sweetheart." He kissed her cheek. "You're prejudiced."

"What I am is a sentimental old fool." Her skirts flared and floated around her big body as she walked toward the door. "I'll wait outside with Benjy."

An hour later, Jacob and Benjy were gliding across the smooth surface of Lake George, searching out the hiding places of all the lake's creatures, while Vashti sat in a folding metal chair on the shore, watching with a maternal and indulgent eye.

"Vashti. Vashti!"

Vashti swiveled her head slowly at the sound of her name being called. Rachel was standing behind her, hair hastily slung into a topknot, sandals still in her hand, and the top button of her blouse unfastened. It was obvious she'd been in a hurry.

"Where's Benjy?"

Vashti nodded toward the distant boat. "Out yonder. With Jacob."

"Jacob!"

"You should have seen their faces—like two peas in a pod. Both of 'em smiling that big wide smile, their eyes kind of crinkled up at the corners. My, my. It did a body good to see them together."

It was suddenly very clear to Rachel how Jacob Donovan had managed to turn up in Florida as her next-door neighbor.

"Well, I suppose Benjy will be safe with him."

"Safe as he would in the front pew of a church. Jacob promised." She nodded toward the other folding chair. "Sit down and relax. This is our vacation. Remember?"

Rachel sank into the chair and leaned down to put on her sandals. "I don't suppose you would know how Jacob Donovan happened to be vacationing here at the same time?"

Vashti chuckled. "I don't suppose you'd be fishing around in that cagey way if you didn't already have your suspicions."

Rachel sat back in her chair, folded her arms over her chest, and waited.

"Now you can get that look off your face," Vashti said.

"What look?"

"You know the one . . . like you're the queen of England and somebody is fixing to be sent to the Tower of London to lose his head. 'Bout time somebody was acting with some sense around here." Vashti reached down for her straw purse and pulled out her fan, buying time. Leaning back in her chair, she looked out over the water, stirring the hot air around with her folding fan. "Of course I called him. From that gas station in Pascagoula. 'Course I did. No use denying the facts."

Rachel squelched the flare of alarm that burst through her. "What facts?"

Vashti studied her face, judging how far she could go and get by with it. "The simple fact is, the two of you never did get over each other, so why keep on running away? Let nature take its course, is what I say."

Rachel's face burned. Nature had already taken its course—last night in Jacob's cabin. And she'd be damned if it would happen again. She couldn't afford to let the needs of her body blind her to the realities of her situation.

"You did the right thing, Vashti."

"What?"

Rachel chuckled. "I surprised you, didn't I? You thought I'd raise Cain about your calling Jacob."

"Ha. It never crossed my mind. You know a good thing when you've got it, and I'm a good thing."

Rachel leaned over and patted her fat arm. "You're a sweet old softy, Vashti, even if you do try to pretend to be such a bossy, hard-headed woman. And I love you as much as I could any mother."

Vashti blinked and swiped at her face. "Bug in my eye," she explained.

"Mine too." Rachel didn't bother to wipe at her tears. Sometimes a woman needed to cry merely to cleanse the soul. "About Jacob. There's no use pretending with you anymore, Vashti. Once I loved him very much, and he'd be so easy to love again. But I can't let myself. There are reasons"—she looked out over the lake at her son and his father. The airboat was coming her way now, cutting through the waters at thirty miles an hour, the airplane motor on the back drowning out the sounds of laughter. She knew they were laughing, for both of them had their heads thrown back. "Reasons I can't discuss," she continued. "There is no need for me to chastise you about calling him. You did what you thought was best." She leaned closer to the old woman, her face earnest. "But you must know this, Vashti. All your matchmaking efforts are a waste of time. Nothing can ever work between Jacob and me."

Vashti merely looked out over the water, nodding and smiling, as if she were carrying on a private conversation in her own head.

Rachel thought it was odd that Vashti didn't try to protest, but she didn't have time to say so. Jacob and Benjy came ashore, laughing and talking at once, like two naughty little boys.

"You should'a seen that alligator. It was bigger than a house."

"At least that big," Jacob added. "Maybe even as big as a barn." The two of them burst into fresh laughter.

"You took my son alligator hunting?"

Jacob sobered. He hadn't known the sight of Rachel would tear a hole in his heart. But it did. After the previous night, nothing would be the same again. They had both said, "Nothing has changed." But it had. Seeing her with the morning sunlight on her hair, with her long legs stretched out, slim and honey tinted, with her eyes still far away and dreamy looking, he almost reeled with desire. His quest for truth faded into the background of his mind, faded so far, it almost vanished.

"The swampy areas around the edge of the lake are teeming with wildlife, Rachel. Not only have we seen alligators, but Benjy and I have seen all kinds of wetland birds." He looked deep into her eyes. "You never know what you'll discover around this lake."

Rachel wanted to run—straight into his arms—but she forced herself to sit quietly in her folding chair.

"It's more fun than the zoo, Mom. Come with us."

Rachel lifted her eyebrows at Jacob for confirmation. His closed expression didn't tell her anything. They gazed at each other for a long while, memories of the night before rising up between them so bittersweet, it hurt.

Benjy tugged her hand. "Will you, Mom? Will you?"

Jacob reached for her other hand. "Come, Rachel. There's room for one more in the boat."

He didn't let her hand go, even after she had risen from her chair.

Vashti watched the two of them walk hand in hand to the water. She noted how he lingered over her, helping her into the boat. She saw the smiles they exchanged, private smiles, like two people in love. Leaning back in her chair, she was content.

As the airboat's motor revved and Jacob pulled it out onto the water, she turned to see a lone green-headed mallard, waddling along the bank, looking for a handout from the tourists. "Seems to me this matchmaking plan of mine is working to a tee, even if I do say so myself. Yessir, seems like things are working out smoother than ice cream on a summer day."

Seven

The boat skimmed the top of the water, parting the marshy grasses at the fringes of the lake. A large bird rose from the bare branches of a dead tree.

"Look," Benjy shouted. "What's that big bird?"

"An osprey." Jacob cut the motor, letting the boat drift, and bent over the little boy in Rachel's lap. "He's a bird of prey."

"He says his prayers?"

"No. It's a different kind of prey. That means he hunts for his food. See how he's circling the water? He's looking for fish. Here. Let me lift you up so you can see better." He took Benjy and held him high, explaining the bird's hunting habits, his nesting preferences, even his different calls.

Benjy asked a dozen excited, little-boy questions. Jacob patiently answered every one. Finally the osprey lifted its great wings and soared far across the lake, out of sight. Jacob settled the boy back onto Rachel's lap.

"Until today, I never knew what I was missing."

Tears formed in her heart, but she didn't dare let them out. "He's a precious child," she agreed.

"I have nieces and nephews, of course, lots of them." He grinned. "And more coming every day. But it must be special, having one of your own."

"It is."

The enormity of what she had done hit Rachel full force. Watching Jacob, she saw exactly how much he would have loved having a child of his own. She'd denied him that. She'd taken six years of his son's life away from him. If he knew . . . if only he knew. . . . She shut her mind to the possibilities.

"I think Benjy's getting sunburned. Could we go back to the cabin for his cap?"

"Certainly. It's almost lunchtime anyhow. How does food sound, sport?"

"Great. My stomach's 'bout to get hungry."

When they got back to the shore, they discovered that Vashti had already gone back to the cabin. Benjy led the way, tugging on Rachel and Jacob's hands.

Jacob glanced across the boy's head at Rachel. "I don't suppose there's any doubt that I'll be staying for lunch."

"You can stay, but we need to talk."

"After lunch. I never could think straight on an empty stomach."

"Con artist."

"I always was, Rachel."

She remembered. She remembered so well. . . .

It had been the day they'd first met. It was January, cold and rainy. They had both been at the Greenville Public Library, Rachel looking for a good mystery novel, and Jacob browsing through the aviation books. He'd spotted her across the stacks.

She saw him coming, red hair all tousled, as if it had been styled by a stiff north wind, and eyes so impossibly blue, she couldn't believe they were real. And that smile. It was as inviting as a hearth fire on a cold winter's day.

He paused, checking the placards on the end of the stacks, then he strolled casually down the narrow aisle toward her.

"Looking for a good mystery?" he asked.

"Yes. It helps pass the time."

"For me, too. Nothing like a good—" he paused, his eyes scanning the book spines, "Agatha Christie to read on a day like this."

"I prefer M. M. Kaye."

"Sure. Him too."

Rachel didn't try to hide her smile.

"You have a beautiful smile." He stuck out his hand. "Jacob Donovan."

"Rachel Windham."

From the moment she'd put her hand in his, she'd known they would be together. Currents of awareness shot through her, so vivid, she felt as if neon lights had been turned on inside her body.

He'd invited her out for hot chocolate. It wasn't until two weeks later that she told him M. M. Kaye was a woman.

Standing on her front porch, watching Vashti escort Benjy to the kitchen, the memories washed over her.

"A penny for your thoughts, Rachel."

She turned and caught Jacob watching her, his face a mixture of puzzlement and vulnerability.

"I was just remembering the first day we met." She smiled. "You pretended to know about mysteries."

He grinned. "It got me what I wanted."

"Only because I wanted it too. In those days, you were quite irresistible, Jacob Donovan."

"Only in those days, Rachel?"

"Last night won't happen again." She hesitated, looking deep into his eyes. There was no sound on the porch. Not even a whisper of a summer breeze marred the deep silence between them.

"It can't happen again," she whispered.

He touched her hair, lightly brushing his fingertips over the shining strands. Her hair seemed to be alive. It caught at his fingers, clung to them, wound around them as if trying to hold on forever.

"I think I'll miss your hair the most, Rachel. . . ." His hand drifted down and cupped the back of her neck. Pulling her close, he pressed his lips briefly against her cheek. "Or perhaps it's the scent of roses I'll miss the most. . . ." He brushed her lips lightly with his. "Or it could be the shape of your lips. . . ." His mouth took hers again, harder this time. "Full and sensual and so right, Rachel, so damned *right*." He tasted her, a light connection of flesh that made her want more.

"You're leaving?"

He captured her lips for one last, fierce kiss, then he released her. Stepping back, he leaned against the porch railing.

"Yes, Rachel, but not because of you."

She fought for control. Had he guessed? she wondered. Did he know?

Jacob started forward. "Are you all right? You're so pale."

She held up her hand. "Don't. I'm all right. Lack of sleep, I guess." Certain her face was not the blank mask she wanted it to be, she turned her back to him.

"You're sure that's all?"

"Yes." She drew a couple of calming breaths before turning to face him again. She even smiled.

Jacob marveled that something as insignificant as loss of color could send him almost into a panic over Rachel. It was a hell of a way to act over a woman he was planning to leave. Exercising some of that iron control he used in fighting a stubborn blaze, he made himself stay against the porch railing, even forced himself to appear relaxed and nonchalant.

"I know I promised to hound your steps until I found out the truth, but I never figured on Benjy."

"I don't want him hurt, Jacob."

"Neither do I, and that's why I'm leaving. I don't want him to become attached to me. I can't be his pal while I'm trying to ferret the truth out of his mother, and then turn my back on him and walk away. I won't do that to your son, Rachel. Even if I never find out the truth."

"Thank you, Jacob."

"Don't thank me yet. I said I was leaving; I didn't say I was giving up."

"Please . . . just let it go."

"No. I can't." He shrugged his shoulders in an eloquent way that was typically Donovan and gave her a debonaire smile. "I guess it's a matter of pride. A man doesn't like to think he let another man win his woman away."

"It wasn't like that, Jacob. You know it."

"No, I don't know it. I know only what you wrote."

"What I wrote was true. I couldn't stand loving a man who might not come home from the next fire or survive the next fast airplane ride."

"I think it was half the truth, Rachel. But that fear doesn't explain why my place in your bed was barely cold before you'd married another."

She paled again. Jacob left his post at the porch railing and chucked her under the chin. "You should try to get more sleep, my sweet." His hand lingered on her face a moment before letting go. "Let's go inside to lunch. I need to say good-bye to Benjy."

"Are you leaving today, Jacob?"

"Is there any special reason I should stay?"

Involuntarily, her gaze swung across the way to his cabin. His low chuckle made her blush.

"Benjy loves the boat so," she said, "and I don't think one more afternoon will make that much difference. Friends come and go in the life of a little boy."

"Tomorrow is soon enough."

He took her arm, and they went inside to lunch.

Jacob had stayed the afternoon, taking Benjy and Rachel out again in the airboat, then he'd said his good-byes. He'd left the lake around nightfall and driven all the way into Orlando for dinner. Ninety miles there and ninety miles back.

Why in the hell wasn't he tired? Why in the hell couldn't he sleep? He kicked back the sheet on his cot and reached for his pants. Maybe some night air would do him good, he thought as he padded barefoot to his front porch.

* * *

In the cabin next door, Rachel peered through the darkness at her clock. Midnight. The last time she'd looked it had said eleven forty-five, and the time before that eleven-thirty. She was exhausted merely from tossing and turning. What was wrong with her? Why couldn't she sleep?

She swung her feet over the side of the bed and into her slippers. Her satin nightshirt whispered against the rumpled sheets as she stood up. Being careful not to wake Vashti and Benjy, she tiptoed through her dark house and onto the front porch. She hoped the night air would clear her head.

Jacob saw her the minute she stepped out onto her porch. The full moon glowed against her hair, reflected off the shiny fabric of her nightshirt.

She leaned against the railing, her long, smooth legs gleaming in the moonlight. Jacob's heart slammed against his chest. Need clambered through his body. Unaware that she was being watched, Rachel stretched her arms high above her head, arching her body in the sensual manner he remembered so well.

"Rachel." He hadn't realized he'd spoken her name until he heard the sound of his own voice. It was too soft for her to hear, of course. If he had to sit out there in the moonlight and make a fool of himself, at least Rachel didn't know it.

Pressing her hips against the railing, Rachel leaned far over her porch and lifted her heavy hair off her neck. It filtered through her fingers, shining like sparklers.

Jacob's chair clattered against the floor as he stood up. His feet padded softly on the wooden steps. The woods were dark and the grass was damp with dew. His mind registered those things, storing them away.

He was moving swiftly now, almost running. His mind noted that too. But it wasn't his mind that was in charge: it was his heart. Rachel was waiting in the moonlight, and he was going to her.

She didn't know what made her turn toward the woods—instinct, a small noise, restlessness. She couldn't be sure. But as her body pivoted slowly, she saw him. Without stopping to wonder why, she left her front porch and walked into the night, toward Jacob.

They met in the middle of the small group of trees. He caught her hands. They exchanged a long, deep look, then Jacob lifted her into his arms and started back to his cabin.

His footsteps sounded like destiny on the porch steps; the slamming of the screen door sounded like fate. Only when they were inside his small bedroom did they speak.

"Once was never enough with you, Rachel."

"It's a good way to say good-bye."

"A very good way."

He lowered her feet to the floor, letting her body slide against his. Her satin nightshirt slithered across his skin, silky and lightly scented. He bent over her and pressed his lips against her throat. Her heavy pulse beat stirred the sweet, heady fragrance so that he seemed surrounded by roses.

"All day I thought of holding you like this." His voice was rich and deep, a husky whisper that tickled her skin.

"And I thought of this, Jacob. . . ." She leaned into his chest. "The way your heart feels against mine."

"Never more than a heartbeat away," he murmured as he took her lips. They were soft and yielding.

He played his mouth tenderly over hers, tasting lightly, sucking briefly, dragging out the heady sweet contact until they both thought the room had tipped upside down. Gone was the sharp struggle of battle they'd known the night before. The crackling feeling of betrayal had vanished. Tonight there was only the tenderness, the coming together of two people who couldn't stay apart.

"Ahhh, Jacob." Rachel tipped back her head, baring her throat. "You whisper through my blood like a blues melody. Hauntingly sweet and almost unbearably sad."

"Sad, my Rachel?"

His lips brushed along the slender line of her throat.

"Seeing you and knowing you can never be mine. That's the sadness."

He ran his hands down her silky back, back and forth, easing away the tension. "Tonight I'm yours." His hands drifted lower until they were cupping her hips. "Tonight you are mine. Only mine."

"Yes." She tangled her hands in his wild hair and pulled his mouth back to hers. The tenderness was edged with hunger now, a fierce longing that grew and grew until it was separate from the two people who kissed, a wild thing, almost out of control.

When he lifted his head, Jacob's eyes were the dark blue of skies before a thunderstorm. "If this is good-bye, I want it to last forever."

"At least until morning comes."

He unbuttoned her nightshirt and slid it slowly over her shoulders. His gaze seared her bare skin, then he bent and planted a long, slow kiss on each shoulder.

"Your mouth is hot, Jacob."

"So am I . . . my Rachel. . . . So am I." He spoke softly, between the kisses he rained gently on her skin.

Her silky nightshirt slipped to the floor. Jacob stepped back and worshiped her with his eyes. She stood very still, letting him memorize her.

"Your breasts are fuller." Reaching out, he cupped one breast.

"Childbirth."

His hands slid downward, causing shivers to skitter along her skin.

"I can still almost span your waist with my hands."

She chuckled, a soft, light sound in the darkness. "Thank you. I work at it."

"The legs . . ." Words failed him. He knelt on the hard wooden floor, letting his caresses do the talking.

His warm breath fanned against her stomach. The need rose high into her throat, making speech impossible. She clutched his shoulders and arched. He met her halfway, and his touch was balm to her soul.

For Rachel, Jacob was all the music she'd ever sung, swirling madly through her body. For him, she was the sky at its most magnificent, wild and beautiful and free. She took him up, higher and higher until he was soaring.

"Jacob." She called his name, shattering the pulsing stillness of the room.

"I'm here, Rachel."

He lifted her onto the cot, lowered her to the sheets with a tenderness beyond imagining. He soothed her with his lips and hands, gentling her, easing her back from the ragged edge of the wild passion that had driven them.

"Easy baby, easy love. The rest of the night is ours."

She pulled him down to her fiercely, as if she could hold back the morning with her passion. At that moment, she didn't want tomorrow to come.

"I want every minute of it with you," she whispered.

His hands separated her legs, lifted her hips. When she was cupped around him, silky and smooth and welcoming, they began the slow, langorous rhythm that would pace them through the night.

As the first blush of dawn glowed against the windowpane, pale gold and soft pink, Rachel stirred in Jacob's arms. He lay on his back, red hair tumbled, eyes closed in sleep. Lifting herself on her elbow, she looked down at him. Her hair made a curtain against his cheek.

She touched his face softly, like the kiss of a summer shower on rose petals. Her hair whispered upon the pillow as she dipped her head down to gaze into his beloved face.

The truth welled up inside her, pushing against the six-year-old barriers. Instinct warred with desire. At that moment, warm with the heat of his body against hers and filled with his seed, she wanted desperately to tell Jacob the truth. She wanted to bare her soul, to confess that he was Benjy's father. The need to tell was so great that she bit her lower lip to keep from waking him up and spilling the truth. Deep down inside her, instinct born of self-preservation warned her to keep quiet. Either way she was doomed. If she kept quiet, as she had all these years, he'd walk away thinking her love hadn't been strong enough. And if she confessed, he'd never forgive her. Never.

She bit her lip so hard she tasted the blood. The truth was best left unsaid.

"Good-bye, my love," she murmured.

Jacob stirred, a smile curving his lips. For a heartbeat, she thought he'd heard. Then he settled back into deep slumber, and she realized he'd only been dreaming.

Bending lower she pressed her lips against his cheek softly, like cloud mists against the sun. Tears blurred her eyes as she rose silently from the bed. It was best to go quickly, she decided as she buttoned her nightshirt. Words wouldn't make any difference. Not now. Not ever. Last night had been their good-bye.

She walked across the room, intending to leave without looking back. When she reached the doorway, she paused, the steady sound of his breathing thundering in her ears. One last look, she told herself. That's all she wanted, all she needed.

The sheet made a tangled loin cloth around his naked body. He was truly splendid lying there, his broad chest and muscled arms as deeply tanned as his face. Even in sleep the laughter couldn't be entirely erased from his face. Laugh lines fanned out from his eyes and humor softened his mouth.

A wave of tenderness swept through her. If ever a man was suited to fatherhood, it was Jacob Donovan. He had such riches to share—a vital, joyous spirit, an infectious laugh, wit and charm and intelligence. She could go on and on, listing his assets. But that didn't outweigh the stark reality: She had kept the most precious gift in all the world from him—his son.

Turning softly so as not to awaken him, she left the room, left the cottage, walking out into the pearly shield of dawn.

• • •

Jacob knew she was gone even before he opened his eyes. He reached for her and clutched only emptiness. Rolling over, he pressed his face into the pillow. The fragrance of roses clung there, the sweet, heady scent that was her signature. He inhaled deeply as if he could bring her back simply by filling himself with her special scent. But no matter how much he wanted her, no matter how real she was in his imagination, his bed remained empty.

With a muttered oath, he kicked the sheet aside and reached for his pants. He would go quickly before he became completely besotted with her . . . again. Rachel was a betrayer; a lovely sorceress who wove her spell and then vanished into the night.

It didn't take him long to pack. Like his sister Hannah, he knew the value of being unencumbered by possessions. Freedom meant flying, and flying was best done without the burden of baggage.

Slinging his duffel bag over his shoulder, he locked the cabin door and bounded down the steps. His hand was on the door of his rented jeep when he heard the sound of laughter. Benjy and Rachel. He turned and looked toward their cabin. They were descending their front steps, hand in hand, laughing together at something one of them had said. An ache rose in Jacob's chest, right around his heart. Across the way stood the woman who had held him captive for six years, the woman who should have been his. And with her was her son, a son who should have also been his. Jacob knew he should turn away; he *wanted* to turn away. But once again his heart ruled his head. He stood in the early morning sun, watching them.

The sounds of laughter floated to him as they bustled back and forth between the cabin and Rachel's car, loading their picnic basket, a blanket, three folding chairs, and every toy Benjy considered necessary for a day's outing. Vashti stood benignly by, sun hat firmly on her head and a smile on her face.

"I bet Jacob would like Magic Mountain."

The excited, little-boy voice carried clearly across to Jacob. They were going to Disney World, he thought. Without him. From now on, everything they did would be without him. The knowledge made him unutterably sad.

As he watched, Rachel bent down and spoke to Benjy, hugging him against her chest. Then she stood and looked toward his cabin, her hand over her heart. He was too far away to see her eyes, too distant to know whether they were bright with tears, but there was something forlorn about the way she stood.

"Good-bye, my love," he whispered. "May the wind be beneath your wings."

As if she had heard him, she straightened her shoulders, tilted her chin at a proud angle, and helped her family into the car. Then they drove off to see Magic Mountain.

There would be no magic for him, Jacob thought as he flung his duffel bag into the jeep, only mountains, and each one steeper and more difficult to climb than the last.

Rachel stayed three more days in Florida. With each passing day, her love for Jacob grew. From the moment he'd sought her out in Biloxi, she'd slowly been coming under his spell. One by one, he'd battered down the barriers she'd erected between them. In his bed, the final barrier had come tumbling down.

His absence served to verify her love. She felt empty without him, lost, restless.

She padded barefoot through the house, softly so as not to wake Benjy from his afternoon nap. "Vashti," she called, "where are you?"

"Out here." Vashti was sitting on the front porch, bent over a piece of needlepoint. She looked up when Rachel came out. "I thought there might be a breeze stirring, but I was wrong. I don't know how that child can sleep in this heat."

"He's young. Children are very adaptable."

"And very wise. The way he took to Jacob . . . my, my. We need never worry about that boy. He can spot character a mile away."

"Vashti—"

Vashti continued, as if she'd never heard Rachel's interruption. "Furthermore, I think Jacob would have stayed if you'd just said the word. Did you see how reluctant he was to leave us? There was something suspiciously like tears in his eyes when he hugged that little boy good-bye. Why, I thought—"

"Vashti!"

Rachel's tone of voice made the old woman look up. Rachel gave her a gentle smile.

"You need not expend your energy promoting Jacob's case. I love him."

"You what?"

"If I ever stopped loving him at all—and I'm not sure I did, even though Bob was a good man and a good husband—I fell in love with him all over again when he came back to Biloxi."

"Nobody is denying Bob's goodness. Lord knows, he did what few men would have done." Vashti, seeing Rachel's eyes widen in shock, hastened to remedy her mistake. "Marrying a woman who obviously loved another man was an uncommon act of bravery."

Rachel calmed herself. There was no reason for Vashti to know the truth. No way she could know. Rachel and Bob had left Greenville soon after the marriage. Vashti, like everybody else, had accepted the story of Benjy's premature birth.

"You're right, Vashti. Bob was uncommonly brave. And he was a good father. For that, I'll always be grateful."

Vashti studied Rachel, opened her mouth to say something, then clamped it shut again. Picking up her needlework, she began to stitch, fast and furiously.

The reticence was so unlike her that Rachel laughed. "Does somebody's life depend on that needlework, Vashti?"

"What?" Vashti's head jerked up.

"Why don't you stop stitching and say what's on your mind. I'm afraid holding it all back will give you ulcers."

"What's on my mind is how come Bob got into this conversation. You told me you love Jacob, but you didn't say what you were going to do about it."

"I guess I was hoping for a little advice."

Vashti didn't try to hide her pleasure. She literally beamed. "From me? You want love advice from me?"

"Who better than you? You have more love in your heart than any person I know. How else could you have sacrificed your own life to raise somebody else's children?"

"Raising you was not a sacrifice, Rachel; it was redemption." Vashti set aside her needlework and leaned back in her chair. "I'm going to tell you a story. . . . I was thirteen when my mother died. Dad took my older brother, explaining to me that boys are easier to handle, and left me in the care of my grandmother. She was in bad health, even then. By the time I was twenty, I was taking care of her. It took all my strength and energy to make a living and watch after Grandma. At least, that's what I thought at the time. When she died, I was forty-two, without much prospects for the future. While I was caring for the sick, life had passed me by. I had no skills except housekeeping and not much education. When I saw Martin Windham's ad in the paper, I felt that fate had smiled on me. The ad had said he wanted a housekeeper, and I was certainly an expert at that. It was not until I came to work my first day that I found out about you. When I saw you peeking around the doorway at me, those big eyes bright with curiosity and that shy smile on your lips, I knew there was a God after all."

"My father didn't even mention me when he hired you?"

"No. He was afraid I wouldn't take the job."

"He viewed me as a burden."

"No, no. It wasn't that. He was a harried, depressed man. His wife was dead and he simply didn't know what to do. Many people are like that, Rachel. They don't know what to do in a particular situation, so they do nothing."

"Thank you, Vashti, for defending my father and for reminding me that I should do something."

Vashti smiled. "You always were a bright girl." She stood up. "I'd better get packing."

Rachel laughed. "Where do you think you're going?"

Vashti gave her a shrewd look. "Unless I miss my guess, we're headed toward Greenville. Seems to me there are a few things you need to tell Jacob Donovan —starting with 'I love you.' "

"That's exactly what I'm going to do. I'm going to tell Jacob Donovan I love him." She felt lighthearted and free for all of two minutes, then her face clouded over. There was something else she had to tell him too.

Jacob knew Rachel was in Greenville two hours after she had arrived. The grapevine was very efficient in a small southern town.

He told himself she was there to visit her father. It was only logical. He told himself her presence in town meant nothing to him. It was a lie.

The minute he saw her, standing in the doorway of the country club, dressed in black, pearls gleaming on her honey-hued skin, he knew he'd been playing mind games with himself. How could she mean nothing to him when merely seeing her made wildfires go rampaging through his body? How could she mean nothing to him when he felt the urge to kill every man who looked at her?

As she glided between the tables, holding her father's arm and smiling like the celebrity she was, he knew beyond a shadow of a doubt that he'd fallen in love with Rachel all over again. He groaned. God help them all.

"Did you say something, Jacob?"

He looked across the table at his sister, Hannah Donovan Roman. Her blue eyes were serene, her dark gypsy hair caught high on her head with a pink ribbon, and her lithe body swathed in a loose-fitting pearly pink dress. She carried her pregnancy well.

"No. I was just commenting on the weather. It's hot."

Hannah tipped back her head and roared with uninhibited delight. "Jacob, you sweet old pretender. You needn't try to fool me. I saw Rachel come through the door."

"No doubt she's visiting her father."

"Are you asking for a confirmation, Jacob?"

"No, that was merely a comment. It's called conversation, Hannah. You and Jim and little Marianne spend so much time in Alaska, you've forgotten what polite conversation is."

Smiling, Hannah leaned back in her chair. "The last time I saw anything as testy as you, I was dealing with a lovesick moose. He thought his lady love was near our cabin, and he uprooted every flower I had before I could convince him to behave."

"And how did you do that?"

"With the business end of a gun, of course. Now he has to wear winter woolens to keep the cold from seeping through the holes in his rump."

Jacob laughed, feeling good. Hannah always made him feel good. "You'll never change, Hannah."

"Jim says he sincerely hopes not."

"And how is the intrepid reporter?"

"Holed up, working fast and furiously on his second novel, and absolutely *dotty* thinking about being a father again. From the way he acts, you'd think he invented fatherhood."

Jacob's glance swung to Rachel. She was leaning toward her father, laughing at something he'd said. Her musical laughter carried across the room.

"Go to her, Jacob."

His head snapped back around toward his sister. "What?"

"I said, go to her." Hannah folded her napkin and placed it beside her plate. "I've finished eating anyway, and I feel the need for an after-dinner nap. I'll take a cab back to the farmhouse."

"You will not. I brought you here, and I'll see you safely home."

"Indulge a pregnant woman, Jacob. If my overly protective husband can trust me to get myself and our daughter safely across the continent for a small visit home, surely you can trust me to take a seven-mile cab ride." She saw that he was wavering, so she went in for the kill. "She's free now, Jacob, and so are you. You might take a lesson from our brother. Tanner would never have found happiness if he hadn't let go of the past." She placed her hand on his arm. "Let it go, Jacob. I want you to be happy."

He leaned over and kissed her cheek. "I'll call you a cab, Hannah."

Rachel watched Jacob escort his sister from the dining room. Disappointment rippled sharply through her.

"I'm glad he's leaving."

She glanced quickly at her father. "Who?"

"Jacob Donovan. You've done nothing but stare at him all evening."

"Dad . . ." She put her hand on his arm. "Please don't start."

"You know how I feel about him. And this latest plan of yours is suicide. I'd absolutely forbid it if I could."

"You can't. He has to know."

"He hasn't had to know for six years. I see no reason to change that now."

"The reason is that I love him." She lifted her chin in defiance. "I've made many mistakes in my life, but none as tragic as what I did to Jacob Donovan. He deserves the truth, even if it means I'll lose him again."

"Is there anything I can say, anything I can do to change your mind?"

"No. I'm going to tell Jacob." She leaned back in her chair, her face as stubborn as her father's.

"Tell me what?"

Jacob's voice, deep and rich and deceptively mild, cut through her consciousness like a steel-edged rapier. Looking up at him, she called on all her professional skills to look serene and happy.

"I was going to tell you that Hannah looks particularly glowing."

Jacob tried to hide his grin over Rachel's bald-faced lie. He'd always admired the way she handled herself when cornered.

"Why, thank you," he said with elaborate politeness. Tearing his gaze away from her flushed and glorious face, he inclined his head toward her father. "Martin. Mind if I join you?" He slid smoothly into the chair beside Rachel, deliberately pulling it close enough so that his thigh touched hers under the table.

Martin didn't try to hide his displeasure. "We thought you were leaving."

"No. There's something I have to do, first." With his leg insistently pressing Rachel's, he leaned back nonchalantly. "When I saw the two of you sitting here, I thought I'd do the neighborly thing and invite you for a ride." A smile tugged at Rachel's lips, and Martin's eyebrows shot up. "An airplane ride," Jacob added smoothly. "It's a beautiful night for flying."

"You must be mad." Martin Windham flung his napkin on the table and stood up. His hostile attitude would have quelled a lesser man. "The only place I'm going is home with Rachel."

Jacob Donovan, who thrived on challenge, was unperturbed by Martin. "I'm sorry you don't want to join us." His emphasis on *us* was not missed by the older man.

Martin glanced toward his daughter, his eyes warning her not to do this foolish thing Jacob Donovan was asking of her, *demanding* of her.

"I'm going, Dad."

To Martin's credit, he didn't protest any further. He knew when he'd been beaten. Pressing his hand tightly on Rachel's shoulder, he leaned down and whispered, "Think carefully before you destroy what you have." Giving Jacob a curt nod of dismissal, he stalked from the dining room.

Rachel's mind and body were both in turmoil, but she covered it with a smile.

"I've missed your smile more than you can imagine." Jacob leaned toward her and lifted her hand to his lips. "Thank you for saying yes."

"If I had said no, would you have abducted me again?"

"It's a temptation, even now."

Her face flushed, she leaned back in her chair, trying to put a comfortable distance between them. In spite of her avowals to confess her love and to tell Jacob the truth, she was afraid. The way she handled telling him would make or break her future.

"But I've already said yes," she added lightly, playing for time.

"The thought of having you slung over my shoulder, at my mercy, has great appeal. I have a sudden desire to make your body burn for me." When he smiled, he was the charming, wicked Irishman she'd fallen in love with so many years ago. She took courage from his smile.

"The last time I was at your mercy, Jacob, it was you who went up in flames."

The bright flush on her cheeks and the sparkle in her eyes told him what he wanted to know, what he'd wondered ever since he'd left that remote cabin on the edge of Lake George. Rachel had not left his bed unscathed. He took hope.

Rising smoothly, he pulled back her chair. When she stood up, he caught her around the waist and pressed her back against him. Her hips molded against his groin made him rigid with desire. He heard her sharp intake of breath.

Leaning down, he whispered in her ear, "Tonight, my sweet, we'll see who burns first." Then, taking her arm and smiling gallantly, as if he had been talking to her about the weather, he sauntered from the dining room.

His car was waiting outside, a fiery red Corvette. Jacob loved fast cars as well as fast planes. Rachel leaned her head against the leather seat, grateful that Jacob hadn't attempted further intimacies. She hadn't expected to see him tonight, and she needed more time to figure the best approach. Saying "I love you" to the man she had jilted years before was not going to be easy. Telling him the truth about his son was going to be even harder. If she told of her love first, would he later accuse of her lying to soften the blow? And if she told him about Benjy first, he probably wouldn't even be around to hear the rest. She sighed.

"Is something troubling you, Rachel?" Steering easily with his left hand, Jacob reached across the seat and caressed her shoulder.

"You've always been sensitive to my moods, haven't you, Jacob?"

His smile was carefree and easy. "It's the Irish in me."

"No. I think it's the tenderness in you."

"Do you find me tender, my sweet?"

"Always. Even when you're striving to be a bastard."

His roar of laughter was her reward. Hearing that great boom of mirth, she relaxed against the seat. Jacob Donovan was not a hard man like her father, she reasoned. Everything was going to be all right.

A comfortable silence descended as the car raced through the warm night. She didn't ask where they were going, and he didn't say. He'd said they would be flying, but knowing Jacob Donovan, that could mean anything. Once he'd told her he was taking her to paradise, and they'd spent all afternoon in bed. She'd thought paradise was the name of one of the out-of-the-way cafés he loved so well.

When they turned underneath the sign that said "Donovan and Company" she turned to him. "Your fire-fighting company?"

"Yes." He drove past a neat concrete and glass office toward a group of hangars. "You trust me, don't you?"

"Yes. I've never stopped trusting you, Jacob."

He shot her a quizzical look.

"Never once," she added. "Not in all the years I've

known you have I ever found you unworthy of my trust. That was never a problem between us."

He smiled. "That's a nice place to start."

He cut the engine and leaned across the seat. Gliding his fingers into her gleaming hair, he cupped her face.

"Tonight is an impulse, Rachel. I had no idea you were coming to Greenville."

"Neither did I."

They looked deep into each other's eyes. Jacob leaned closer until their lips were almost touching. But he knew that if he started kissing her now, he would never stop. And as much as he wanted to make love to her, he wanted more to say what was on his mind.

Still holding her face, he said, "When I heard you were in town, I told myself I didn't care."

"Did it work?" she whispered.

"No."

"It never has for me either."

His lips brushed her forehead. "You've told yourself you didn't care?"

"For years." He laid his cheek against her hair. They were silent while the night sounds beat around them—the distant sounds of traffic on the highway, the singing of crickets in the bushes, the whining of the ever-present mosquitoes in the sultry delta.

Rachel broke the silence. "Finally, it didn't work anymore, Jacob. After you left Florida, I knew I had to come to you."

"Why, Rachel?" He pulled back and watched her closely. He needed to see her face. When she said the words he hoped to hear, he needed to see the truth in her eyes. Long ago, love was something he'd accepted automatically, almost as his due. He was older now and far, far wiser. Six years without hope tended to make a man cynical, he thought.

When she hesitated, he caught her gently at the nape, massaging his fingers into her soft skin.

"I want to hear the words, Rachel. Why did you follow me to Greenville?"

"Because I love you." She saw the joy flicker across his face, watched the flame leap in his eyes. And she was filled with hope. "I never stopped loving you, Jacob. Not even in all the years we were apart."

He couldn't trust himself to say anything yet, so he held onto her, almost afraid to let go for fear she'd vanish.

"If that seems disloyal to Bob, perhaps it is. But it's the truth, and I can no longer avoid the truth." She reached for him, touching his face in a gesture that begged his understanding. "My marriage was one of comfort and convenience. It was a rescue mission by a dear man for a confused young woman."

Jacob waited, listening.

"I married Bob knowing I loved you, and for that I can only beg your forgiveness."

"And Bob?"

"He understood. I'm asking you to do the same thing."

"Say the words again."

"I love you, Jacob Donovan."

His hand trembled on her neck. She saw the desire in his eyes and the effort it cost him not to give in to that desire. She hadn't expected more. Jacob's easygoing, fun-loving ways might fool some people, but they didn't fool her. She knew him too well. He was a man who had pitted his courage and steely determination against blazing holocausts time and time again, and had walked away the winner.

Besides all that, Rachel was too practical to think that six years of alienation and pain could be wiped away by three simple words. Right now Jacob's hand, massaging the back of her neck, was the only reassurance she had.

The silence stretched between them until she felt as if her nerve endings were screaming. At last, Jacob spoke.

"I do my best thinking in the sky. Come."

Taking her hand, he led her into a vast, dark hangar. Jacob flipped a switch, and light flooded the area. His twin-engine Baron was there parked beside a smaller, single-engine Cessna. In one corner was a huge multicolored balloon, deflated beside its woven basket. The jet he used to transport his equipment to oil field fires was also there.

"Where's your P-Fifty-one Mustang?"

"You know about that plane?"

"Yes. I kept up."

Gladness filled his heart, but it was too early to let it show. Once burned, twice shy, he decided.

"Rick has it." He saw no need to tell her why. After tonight, he hoped it wouldn't matter anymore. He would call Rick and tell him the investigation was off. He loved Rachel, and that's all that mattered. Her reasons for marrying another man were no longer important.

"We'll take the Cessna tonight." He lifted her into the plane. "You're not afraid, are you?"

"Not anymore."

He smiled down at her. "You're sure?"

"I confess to a few butterflies in my stomach, but that could be love."

His laughter filled the hangar as Jacob climbed into his plane.

He taxied the Cessna along the runway, the engine roaring and the tires singing. Fingers of fear clutched at Rachel's stomach, and then the plane was lifting proudly, higher and higher into the vastness above them. She turned to watch Jacob. His profile was beautiful, chiseled against the backdrop of stars and sky. All the love he felt for flying was clearly evident on his face.

Rachel leaned back in her seat, content. If Jacob could only love her *half* that much, that's all she'd ever need to make her the happiest woman on earth.

She reached to touch him.

Eight

The Cessna cut through the night sky, climbing toward a towering bank of clouds.

"There's something I want to show you, Rachel." Jacob fell silent as he piloted the plane into the fuzzy gray clouds.

Instead of watching the clouds, Rachel watched Jacob. He was totally at ease and supremely in command.

"You love it, don't you?"

He smiled at her. "I love it so much that I pity earthbound mortals."

The plane lifted through the cloud cover and into starlight. After the foggy darkness, the stars were almost blinding.

"Look above us, Rachel."

She glanced out the window, craning her neck to look up. Above them was another layer of clouds, so thick and heavy, they looked as if they might fall down and engulf the small plane.

"Cloud banks above and below. We're going to

travel down this avenue of stars. And if we're lucky—" Jacob broke off, staring intently out the window. "There." He pointed straight ahead. "See it, Rachel?"

A great shining silver orb floated up out of the clouds below them, drifting slowly among the stars.

"It looks like a UFO, Jacob."

He laughed. "Many flyers mistake it for that when they first see it."

"It's awesomely beautiful."

"Only those of us who dare to challenge the skies ever get to see the moon rising between two cloud banks. It's a sight of such power and mystery that it makes our small strivings seem insignificant."

"I envy the moon."

"Why?"

"I've always known you were a poetic man. I used to see that side of you when we made love. But it's this—" she paused, her hand sweeping the heavens, "that brings out the poetry in you. The sky is your first love."

Her eyes were bright as she turned to him. The moon was forgotten as they gazed at each other. Quietly, Jacob put his plane on automatic pilot. Leaning over, he unbuckled Rachel's seat belt. Words weren't necessary. He circled her waist and lifted her onto his lap.

She caught his face between her hands. "Kiss me, Jacob. Love me."

He pressed his hands against hers. "I thought I would never say this to you again, Rachel . . . I never thought a second chance was possible for us. . . ." Now that she was there in the sky with him, now that he was holding her in his arms, words came slowly for him. "It's been so long. . . ."

"I'm here. I'm listening."

"I love you, Rachel. Lord knows, I tried not to. I fought against loving you again as hard as I've ever battled against an oil field fire. But this is one battle I couldn't win—didn't want to win." His hand circled her nape, his fingers tangling into her silky hair as he pulled her closer. "You are my first love. The heavens are nothing compared to you. It's you I love, Rachel. . . . Only you," he murmured. His mouth closed over hers.

Rachel thought fleetingly of the secret she was still hiding, then her thoughts went winging away toward the heavens, borne upward by the beauty of Jacob's kiss.

He parted her lips, sliding his tongue into her mouth. She received him joyously. All the barriers were down, the shields were lowered, the battlements breached. This time no one was the conqueror and no one the conquered. They both surrendered to love.

Jacob moaned in his agony of need. His hands slid over her body, tormenting, seducing, until Rachel lost all control.

"Jacob . . . oh, yes, Jacob . . . take me."

In the small confines of the pilot's seat, they were clumsy. Their hands fumbled on zippers, tangled in the silky folds of her dress. And when Rachel was wearing only high heels and pearls, she enfolded Jacob in her welcoming warmth.

"Ahhhh, Rachel." He thrust his hips upward, plunging deeper until he was fully sheathed within her. "To have you here is a dream beyond imagining." His hands caressed her satiny back, moved upward to tangle in her perfumed hair. "Are you cold, love?"

"I'm hot. . . . You . . . make . . . me . . . burn." Her words were short breathy explosions.

Together they soared. Imprisoning her lips with his, Jacob took his Rachel. With a wild and carefree abandon, he plunged, each stroke making his heart swell with joy. Her nails dug into his back; her hips arched, meeting each thrust with a stormy passion that had him groaning.

Even the pearls around her neck grew hot.

"You . . . make . . . me . . . wild . . . my Rachel. . . ."

She felt the damp sheen on the bunched up muscles of his back. Lowering her head, she licked at the moisture with her tongue.

His rhythm increased. The small Cessna bucked under them.

"Us?" she murmured against his burning skin.

"Air pockets. . . ." His voice became a husky moan as her mouth seared up the side of his neck. Her tongue circled his lobe, then plunged inside his ear.

Jacob drove fiercely into her. Ecstasy rippled through her body. She heard a sound from far off, unaware that it was her own voice calling his name. Convulsions of pleasure racked her, and Jacob's arms tightened.

His body exploded, pouring his seed into her with a force that tore her name from his chest. "Rachel, my Rachel."

She put her hand on his damp brow and tenderly pushed back his hair. "I'm here, Jacob. I'll always be here for you."

"Is that a promise?"

"A sacred vow."

He bent over her and kissed the hot pearls at her throat.

"I've always loved you in pearls, my sweet."

Holding her against him, his flesh still encased in hers, Jacob took control of his plane. He banked to the left and set a course back to Greenville. Rachel leaned her head on his chest, content to be in the sky with the man she loved.

The earth came up to meet them as they descended. Still holding Rachel, Jacob touched down and taxied down the runway. Only when they had come to a complete stop did Rachel leave his lap and put on her clothes.

Sitting in the dark cockpit, he smiled at her. "I'm only going to take them off again."

"I was hoping you'd say that."

They locked the plane in the hangar, got into Jacob's Corvette and drove to his house. It was made of natural stone and glass, nestled among the giant oak trees that bent their branches over the river. Jacob's house was like everything else about him, spare and clean and intensely masculine.

Standing in the hallway with the stars shining through the skylight, Rachel looked at Jacob. "I like your house. It suits you."

He touched her hair. "It's been lonesome. Only you can make it a home."

He picked her up and carried her to his bedroom. The room was spacious and airy, with moonlight spilling across the thick carpet. His bed was on a dais facing a large bank of windows that overlooked the river. Cascades of moonlight poured through skylights.

Jacob placed her on his bed, watching her glorious hair spread over his pillows.

"You belong here, my love."

"I want to belong here."

He undressed her almost reverently, peeling away the silken layers until she lay naked upon his bed.

The pearls gleamed softly at her throat. Leaning down, he kissed them one by one.

Each touch of his lips branded her. Time went spiraling away as Jacob and his Rachel loved. Each time she sought to reveal her secret, he hushed her with another kiss.

Together they watched the sun rise over the river, and then Jacob drove her to her father's house.

She trailed her fingers across his cheek, reluctant to bid him good-bye. He softly kissed her mouth.

"We'll talk, Rachel. I'll call you later in the day."

"I'll be waiting."

He got out of the car and escorted her to her front door. Cupping her face, he gave her one last fierce kiss. "I love you. Remember that. I love you."

"Jacob . . . there are things I must tell you."

He put his finger on her lips. "Shhhh. The past doesn't matter anymore. My quest for the truth has ended with you. Nothing matters except you." His hands tightened on her face. "Say it. I want to hear you say it one more time."

"I love you, Jacob. I'll always love you."

She turned from him, and then she was gone. He thought there were tears in her eyes when she went inside. The skin at the back of his neck prickled. Premonition. Martin would give her a hard time. He put his hand on the door and almost followed her, then he chided himself for being foolish. Martin had been unusually brusque at the country club, but then he had always been a hard man. And he'd never liked Jacob's profession any more than Rachel had. He was probably just being an overprotective parent.

Jacob went down the front steps and drove off into the new morning.

* * *

The jangle of the telephone woke him. Struggling out of a deep sleep, he peered at the clock. One P.M. He'd eaten a logger's breakfast and then tumbled into bed after he'd driven Rachel home. He was still groggy and pleasantly exhausted. It was going to take him a long time to make up for six years of being deprived of Rachel. He'd tried to do it all in one night.

Smiling, he picked up the receiver.

"Jacob Donovan," he said.

He listened to the caller. His body began to tense, his adrenaline to flow. It was a distress call—an oil field fire in Venezuela, raging out of control. Jacob and his special fire-fighting team were being asked to come in and contain the blaze.

He reacted immediately. There was no time to lose. First he called his office, instructing his team to start loading the jet. Next he placed a call to Seattle. Rick McGill, his right-hand man, had last called him from there.

"Rick, there's been a well blowout in Venezuela."

"How bad?"

"Bad. It's been going for three days. Two men killed and six severely burned."

"Damn! What ignited it, Jacob?"

"Some fool smoking around the rig. He had a cigarette in his hand when the blowout started. The foreman said they thought the preventer would stop the blowout. When they saw it wasn't working, they started running. By then the gas was coming up from the well. One spark from the cigarette, and you know the rest."

"Yeah. The well is now a blowtorch, burning everything in its path." Rick sounded depressed.

"We'll handle it, Rick. We always have."

"Sure. I'm on my way now."

"You might as well meet us in Venezuela. No point in us waiting for you to get here first." Jacob gave him precise directions.

"See you there, Jacob."

Jacob made his last call to Rachel.

"I have to be brief, sweet," he told her. "There's a fire in Venezuela, just south of Maracaibo."

"How soon are you leaving?"

"As soon as we can get the equipment loaded."

"May the wind be beneath your wings, Jacob." She automatically used his favorite parting phrase. "I love you."

As soon as she hung up, Rachel covered her face with her hands. Terror ripped through her. The man she loved was going straight into a fiery holocaust. Each day he was in Venezuela, his life would be in danger. She groaned in agony.

"Rachel? Rachel, honey. What's the matter?"

She turned to see Vashti hurrying toward her.

"It's Jacob. He's been called to Venezuela."

"Fighting a fire?"

"Yes."

Vashti folded Rachel to her bosom. Crooning the way a mother does to a small child, she smoothed Rachel's hair.

"It will be all right. You just wait and see."

"I love him, Vashti." Rachel's voice was muffled against her shoulders.

"I know you do. I *know* you do."

"But I never got a chance to—" Realizing what she'd been about to say Rachel stopped herself.

Vashti held her at arm's length. "To tell him he's Benjy's father?"

Rachel gasped. "How did you know?"

"Honey, I knew you were pregnant before you did. Don't you think I could see what was happening to my child? That morning sickness, those buttons you loosened on your skirt band. I kept quiet all these years, hoping and hoping." When Rachel's tears started, Vashti pulled her close again. "Hush now, hush, baby. You'll get that chance to tell him. Everything's gonna be all right now. It's gonna be all right."

Jacob and his team had been battling the blaze for five days. They were soot-blackened and exhausted. Most of the outlying fires had been contained with chemical foam, but the gas pocket deep in the earth's strata continued to spew forth from the well.

The team worked around the clock in shifts, but Jacob took off only a few hours at a time, covering his exhaustion with crisp commands and a brisk, positive attitude. His men counted on him for leadership, and he gave it to them.

"Jacob, you've been out here for the fourteen hours. Why don't you take a break?" Jacob peered through the asbestos shield that covered his face. He'd never seen Rick so worried and uptight.

"Are you reminding me that I'm only human, Rick?"

"Somebody has to do it."

Jacob rubbed the back of his tired neck. "You're right. I need a break."

He placed his second-in-command, Charlie Macanaw, in charge and left the site with Rick. They drove to the group of tiny shacks that served as housing for them and the men who crewed the drilling rigs. In the distance, the glow of the blazing fire lit up the night.

They pulled off their outer gear and sank onto the narrow bunks. The two of them were sharing the primitive accommodations.

"You've been lower than a toad these last few days. Chin up," Jacob said. "We've handled worse."

"It's not the fire that's bothering me."

"What then?" Jacob shoved a pillow behind his back and looked over at his friend.

"It's that investigation. I've been waiting for a chance to tell you what I've found out, and now that I have it, I'll be damned if I know how."

Jacob tensed Prickles of alarm crawled through his belly. His throat got tight.

"Rick, every time we've taken a break during these last five days, I meant to tell you . . . it doesn't matter anymore. Rachel's reasons for marrying Bob aren't important. I love her. I never stopped."

"Damn!" Rick jumped up from his bunk and began to pace the floor, striking his fist into his palm.

Jacob squelched the fear that threatened to suffocate him.

"That's not the reaction I expected." He tried for a smile that didn't quite work. "Congratulations are usually in order."

Rick's shoulders sagged. His feet planted wide in a fighter's stance, he stopped in the middle of the room. "Does Rachel return your love?"

"She does. She's told me so in a dozen different ways." Jacob smiled. "All of them wonderful."

"What else has she told you?"

Jacob gave Rick a sharp glance. "Is there anything she should tell me?"

"I suppose that's for her to decide." Rick resumed his pacing.

Jacob got off his bunk and put his hand on Rick's shoulder. "You might as well tell me what's bothering you and get it off your chest."

"You said you didn't want to know."

"If you were in my place, would you want to know?"

Rick didn't hesitate. "Hell, yes."

Alarm squeezed Jacob's heart again. Forcing himself to appear lighthearted, he sat on the edge of the bunk.

"I guess I'd better be sitting down when you tell me."

Rick faced his friend. "Bob Devlin was not Benjy's father," he said quietly.

A silent scream of agony exploded in Jacob's head. Pain ripped his heart. The words roared around his mind, whirling with the devastating power of a tornado, blowing away his love, his happiness, his chance for a future. He felt numb all over.

"Are you sure?"

"Positive."

"How do you know?"

"Benjy was born in a private clinic owned by Martin Windham less than seven months after Rachel's wedding. There were no other patients there. A shroud of secrecy surrounded the birth. And, of course, Rachel and Bob never lived in Greenville after the child was born. The story was that Benjy was premature. It might have worked except for the accident."

Jacob was silent. Each word his friend spoke was a hammer blow to his heart.

Rick took a deep breath and continued. "It happened when they were living in Seattle. Benjy was on an outing with a church group. The roads were icy. The bus swerved off the road and plunged down an embankment. Benjy lost a lot of blood, so much that his father was called in to donate."

"The blood didn't match?"

Rick sank onto his own bunk, defeated. "There was no way in hell Bob Devlin could have fathered Benjamin."

Jacob's eyes were haunted as he looked across at his friend. "You were right. This is something I wanted to know. I can't say the possibility never crossed my mind, though." He stood up slowly, as if the weight of the last six years were crushing him. "I need to be alone for a while."

"I'll bunk in with Jack and Mick."

Rick left the small shack quickly. He'd gone only three feet from the front door when he heard the crash. Tin clattering against the wall.

"There goes the water pitcher," he muttered.

A second loud crash quickly followed by another announced the demise of a couple of chairs. Next came the cry of agony, so desolate it made the hairs on Rick's neck stand on end. Then there was silence.

He started to go back into the shack, but Jacob had asked for privacy. He had to respect that. His heart ached for his friend as he made his way through the dark.

Jacob grieved. His shoulders shook with silent tears as he mourned the lost years. Benjamin was his son, and he'd never been there to hold him when he'd cried, to see his first smile, to watch him take his first step, to hear him say his first word. Rachel had denied him that. She'd taken it all away with her lies.

On the heels of his grief came rage so cold and bitter, it made him shiver, even in the sultry heat. He sat on his bunk far into the night, staring into the dark.

•   •   •

One week after Jacob left for Venezuela, Rachel knew she couldn't stand the waiting any more. She told her father good-bye, drove Vashti and Benjy back home to Biloxi, and caught a plane to South America. Jacob had said he'd be somewhere south of Maracaibo. An oil field fire shouldn't be too hard to find.

The atmosphere in Maracaibo was festive. Dancers wearing colorful masks blocked traffic. Music and laughter filled the streets.

Rachel leaned over the front seat of her taxi and spoke to the driver.

"Can't we go any faster?"

He gave her a wide, toothless grin. "No, señorita. If we go fast, we roll over six, maybe seven dancers. Make flat, like tortilla." The taxi swerved and rocked as he took his hands off the wheel and slapped his hands together, demonstrating how flat he would make the dancers. Laughing at his own humor, he grabbed the wheel. "We crawl, eh? We pinch along like bugs. Some day soon we get where we going—when carnival is over, eh?"

Rachel chuckled. She didn't like to "pinch" along, but it was better to laugh than cry, she thought. She supposed she should be thankful for small favors. At least the taxi driver spoke English, such as it was. Her Spanish would have been even worse.

It took her four hours to get to the site of the oil field fire. Black smoke billowed into the sky; flames crackled and roared, shooting upward, raining sparks and cinders. The entire area seemed to be a mass confusion of asbestos-suited men and noisy machines.

Rachel fought back the panic that threatened to swamp her. Somewhere out there was Jacob. The man she loved was in the midst of that towering inferno.

"Carumba," the taxi driver said. "You want to go *there*?"

"Yes."

He began to mutter in rapid Spanish. The only word Rachel caught was loco. She supposed she was. She guessed that all people in love were a little crazy.

"Can we go closer?"

The driver pointed straight ahead. "No. Security."

"I'll go on foot from here."

Shaking his head in disbelief, the driver collected his cab fare. Extortion, Rachel thought as she counted out the money. But seeing Jacob was worth any price.

As the cab driver drove back toward Maracaibo, Rachel picked up her small bag and started toward the security guard. He could tell her where Jacob was staying. She remembered from their conversations of years gone by that he always had some sort of lodging near the site of the fires. She also knew that he would be there only rarely, but that didn't matter. If she could have five minutes with him, she'd be satisfied.

The security guard spoke no English, but Rachel managed to communicate. What she couldn't say in Spanish, she made up for with eloquent gestures and a smile. The guard fell under her spell. Not only did he explain that Jacob Donovan was out there in the midst of the fire, but he also loaded Rachel's bag into his jeep and drove her to the small shack where Jacob was staying.

She thanked the guard and sat down on the narrow bunk to wait.

· · ·

Rachel waited for three hours. Darkness had come suddenly, dropping over the small shack like a shroud fallen from the sky.

She spun toward the door at the sound of footsteps. "Jacob!"

Rachel hurried toward him, arms outstretched. He stood just inside the door. In his smoke-streaked face, his eyes were incredibly blue and filled with such cold fury that she faltered. Her steps slowed and she lowered her arms. She'd guessed he might be angry that she had come without telling him, but she'd never dreamed he'd be so furious.

"I know I should have let you know I was coming. . . . I know it's a terrible time for you."

"Do you, Rachel?" He walked past her, jerking off his fire-fighting clothes as he stalked across the room.

"Of course. I saw the fire. It must be horrible, going there every day, never knowing what will happen next."

"The fire is nothing compared to the hell I'm going through."

Rachel felt the first cold fingers of fear raking along her nerve endings. She watched him hang up his gear. He moved carefully and precisely, as if he were a high explosive that could go off at any minute. The stiffness of his back was eloquent testimony to his tight control.

She folded her hands tightly together and waited. When he turned around, his face was rigid with tension. "That's a nice act you have, Rachel—pretending to love a man." He jerked a chair back from the table and sat down. "You're good. You're damned good. You had me fooled."

Rachel forced herself to remain calm. "I love you, Jacob," she said quietly.

His piercing blue eyes sought hers. For the first time in her life, Jacob's gaze made her shiver with fear. He knew, she thought. Somehow he'd found out. She held her head up, bearing his cold scrutiny with all the dignity and control she could muster.

She saw the emotions war across his face—anger, love, betrayal, confusion. At last he stood up and pulled back a chair.

"Do sit down, Rachel," he said with elaborate politeness. "I hate to sit while a lady is standing." The scathing emphasis he put on *lady* chilled her heart.

He held the chair for her while she sat, playing his role of gallant Southern gentleman to the hilt. But he was scrupulously careful not to touch her. When he took his seat across the table, she started talking.

"Jacob . . . when you left Florida, I realized that I could no longer keep the truth from you. I went to Greenville with the specific purpose of telling you why I married Bob Devlin. But you were called away to this fire. . . ."

"How very convenient for you, Rachel."

"Please don't do this to us."

"Don't do what? It seems you've already done it all—lie, cheat, steal." He leaned back in his chair, his face a blank mask. "Does that about cover everything, my sweet?"

Never had an endearment sounded so horrible. Rachel prayed for the right words to break through his terrible wall of fury. She prayed for the strength to endure and the wisdom to triumph.

"It wasn't like that, Jacob."

"How was it, Rachel?" He leaned across the table and stared into her eyes. "Tell me all the noble reasons you had for stealing my son."

Her head snapped up. She *would not* cringe before Jacob Donovan.

"He's my son too. And I was the one who was pregnant when you left for Saudi Arabia. I did what I thought was best at the time. Maybe it was a mistake, but—"

"A *mistake!*" He rose from his chair and stalked around the table, towering over her. Reaching down he gripped her chin. "Look me in the eye and tell me how you could deprive me of my son and call it a mere *mistake.*"

She jerked out of his grasp and stood up to face him. "Call me a coward, Jacob. I was young and pregnant and scared, and I made the wrong decision. But I am not a heartless monster. I never deliberately set out to deprive you of Benjamin."

"Well, you did a damned good job of it." He gripped her shoulders. She could feel his fingers biting into her flesh, but she didn't flinch. "Dammit all, Rachel, you even gave him another man's name."

"Bob loved Benjy. He was a good father."

"He was a good father to *my* son." Jacob released her and strode across the room. She could see his muscles bunch up under his shirt as he stared out the small window at the darkness.

She wanted desperately to go to him, but she knew that now was not the time. Before she touched him, she had to let Jacob vent his wrath.

"If it makes you feel any better, I've borne the burden of this guilt for six years."

He turned slowly around, his hands crammed deep into his pockets. "Guilt becomes you, Rachel. It has made you more radiant . . . and more lethal."

"I didn't mean to fall in love with you again, Jacob. When you came back to Biloxi, I fought against it."

"And when you realized I was getting close to the truth, you confessed your undying devotion in order to protect your beautiful hide."

"No." Her own anger was welling up against his implacable will. "You know that's not true."

"Do I?"

She lost control. Her shoes slapped sharply against the wooden floor as she ran across the room. She caught his shoulders and glared at him, eye to eye. "Damn you, Jacob Donovan. What we had in that Cessna was not pretense. Don't you dare make something ugly of something that was so beautiful and precious. Don't you dare!"

Jacob felt the heat of his passion rising, and he was astonished. Rachel had cut cleanly through his wrath and grabbed him by the heart—just as she always had. He called upon every reserve of will he had to fight his raging desire. But it was a losing battle.

"I loved you then, and I love you now," she said. "You can't deny that."

He pulled her roughly against him. "Show me, Rachel. Make me see how beautiful it was."

Knowing he couldn't help himself, he slammed his mouth down on hers. She met his punishing lips with a fierceness of her own.

She felt his heart pounding heavily against hers; she heard the ragged racing of his breath. The bruising, brutal kiss went on and on until she almost swooned for lack of air.

When he finally lifted his head, his eyes were bright and deadly.

"Is that love, Rachel?"

"No, Jacob." Her voice was soft as she put her hands on his chest. She circled her hands tenderly over that broad expanse, and then she began to unbutton his shirt. "But this is." She parted the shirt and pressed her lips against his skin. Her tongue darted among the crisp hairs.

Jacob tried to steel himself against her touch. His mind screamed with all the things he'd called her the last two days—betrayer, liar, thief. But nothing worked. She was a witch, and he fell under her spell.

Passion raged in him, stoked by her caresses and his consuming wrath. He jerked off his clothes and sent them flying across the room. A small sane corner of his mind screamed "Stop!" But it was too late. Rick would be out at the fire all night, and Rachel was there, ready and willing and so sensual, she turned the whole shack into a blazing conflagration.

Rachel came to him naked. He hadn't even been aware of the moment she'd shed her clothes. He moved his hands roughly over her body. He wanted to control her, possess her, punish her. Every inch of her tender flesh claimed his attention. He sought with mouth and tongue to brand her. He took her breast deep in his mouth, sucking until she was moaning, begging him for more.

Suddenly he lifted her and carried her to the bed. The ancient springs groaned under their weight. Silently, he placed her on the sheets and drove into her. She caught the headboard and took him, fully and completely.

There were no love words spoken. No soft murmurings accompanied their joining. It was not love they made; it was war.

They stayed locked in passionate combat for an hour. Rachel sought to heal by giving, and Jacob sought to punish by taking.

When it was over, Jacob rolled off her and stood up. Looking down at her tousled beauty, he felt nothing. Not love, not sorrow, not regret. He was still as empty as he had been the day Rick had told him that Benjamin Devlin was his son.

"You can stay here tonight. Rick won't be coming back." His voice was cold and curt. "Tomorrow you can leave." He turned to go.

"Jacob. . . ." Propping herself on her elbow, she caught his hand. "Where are you going?"

His eyes blazed down at her. "To hell." He jerked on his pants and walked out the door. It banged shut behind him.

Silent tears ran down Rachel's face. "Forgive me, my love," she whispered. "Forgive me."

But nobody was there to hear.

Jacob walked blindly in the darkness. He had no timetable, no destination. And then he was running, running as far away from Rachel as he could. He ran for an hour, for two. He didn't know how long. The darkened shacks were a blur to him. The forest rose up beside him, unnoticed. Even the brightness from the distant fire failed to catch his attention. At last, exhaustion forced him to stop.

He sank beside the road and put his head in his hands. Shame poured through him. For the first time in his life he had used a woman. And not just any woman. Rachel. He had tried to bury his hatred in the torrid flesh of the woman he loved.

His body jerked. Not love, his mind screamed. He didn't love her anymore. She'd destroyed all that. He lifted his fist and shook it at the moon. The moon had no right to be so beautiful when his life was so ugly and wretched.

He rose slowly and started back to the encampment. He was bone weary, and his time was limited. He'd squandered too much already. He couldn't afford to go back to the fire without any sleep. Too many lives depended on him.

When he got back to the shack, Rachel was sleeping. In the pale light that filtered through the windows he could see a tear that was not yet dry on her cheek. Remorse shot through him.

Bending down, he touched his lips to her temple. It was damp with sweat.

"I'm sorry, Rachel," he whispered.

The faint scent of roses drifted around him.

Nine

The sound was soft—a footstep on the floor—but it brought Rachel completely awake. She sat up, pulling the sheet over her breasts, and watched Jacob dress. It was not quite dawn.

He hadn't noticed her yet, and he was taking great care not to awaken her. She almost smiled. She'd never seen a big man tiptoe. As he pulled on his pants and shirt, she thought of the many other times she'd watched him dress. Happy times. Jacob had always been laughing and joking about how he needed her help. He'd cajole her out of a warm bed with his smile, then they would both be right back under the covers, tangled together in his shirt and giggling as only people in love can.

She wished she had some magic to bring back the past. Propping her elbow on her knees, she feasted her eyes on him.

A sense of being watched made Jacob spin around. When he first saw her, with her tumbled hair and love-flushed face, he felt a surge of joy. Then the ugly truth came pouring through him.

"Rachel." He nodded curtly toward her, as if he were acknowledging a stranger. "I'm glad you're awake."

His cold tone squashed any hope she might have had.

"We need to talk, Jacob."

His smile was bitter. "Yes, we do. But I think it's best if you stay on that side of the room, and I stay on this side. We always seem to get sidetracked."

She hugged her knees, taking courage from the solid feel of her own flesh. "I won't make excuses for what I did, Jacob. All I can do is ask for your forgiveness and hope for your understanding."

Forgiveness doesn't come easily for a man with a raw and gaping wound. Jacob knew that and accepted it. At the moment he thought forgiveness might never come.

"You want me to absolve you of guilt and let you get on with your life. Is that about it, Rachel?"

"No. I want you in my life."

"You want a miracle."

"You could say that. I love you, Jacob. I want you to know that."

"You're a great actress. You almost make me believe you."

"It's not like that!" She swung her feet over the side of the bed. The sheet slipped down from her breasts.

"Stay where you are." Jacob stalked across the room and jerked up the sheet. Lifting Rachel by the shoulders, he wrapped the sheet around her. "Keep that damned sheet on and don't move." Turning around, he stalked to the other side of the room and sat down.

"Tell me about my son, Rachel."

"What do you want to know?" She sat on the edge of the bed.

"What was the first word he spoke? Who was there to see him take his first step? Did he cry at night, and who comforted him if he did? Who read bedtime stories to him? Was it Bob? Did Bob Devlin do all those things for my son?"

Rachel met the cold fury in his eyes with a level gaze. "His first word was baba. That's baby talk for bottle. Food was infinitely more fascinating to him than either of his parents." She realized her mistake when she saw the way his face darkened.

"Go on."

"He's always had a sunny disposition. He never cried at night unless he was wet or hungry. We were both there for him, Jacob. Even though Bob knew Benjy was your son, he loved him as devotedly as if he had been the natural father."

"He'd damned well better have."

"Vashti was there too. She and I took turns reading the bedtime stories. As Bob's health failed, he felt less and less like taking time with Benjy. But Benjy was always loved, Jacob."

"It shows. He's a great kid." Jacob stood up. "I intend to be a part of my son's life, Rachel."

"He's just a little boy!" Holding her sheet around her, she jumped up from the bed and whirled to face him. "I won't let you embroil him in a nasty legal battle."

Jacob came toward her and gripped her shoulders. Hauling her close, he glared into her face. "Do you think I'd do that to my son? Do you think I'd hire lawyers and treat him like a piece of property?"

She looked into his eyes and saw the pain. "No, Jacob," she said quietly. "You're much too kind and generous to do that to Benjy."

He released her and stepped back. In the face of her reasonableness, his rage began to ebb. "You and I can work out the details when I get back to the States. The only advice I want from professionals is in knowing the right time to tell Benjy I'm his father."

"I've thought of that too."

Her reply took him by surprise. "You have?"

"Yes. Over the years I came to realize that I had denied Benjy the right of knowing what a wonderful man his natural father is. He deserves to know his bloodlines, his ancestry." The sheet trailed behind her as she walked to the window. Pale fingers of light were beginning to brush across the horizon. "Children are very adaptable, Jacob. I will work with you on this." She turned from the window to face him.

"Rachel"—Jacob started to reach out, and then he lowered his hand—"I'm sorry for last night. There's no excuse for the way I treated you. All I can do is promise you it won't happen again."

"You were hurting."

"I still am."

"So am I."

"Every time we come together, we make a mess of things, don't we?"

"We're only human, Jacob."

Jacob realized that the soul-blistering wrath he'd felt was gone. His shoulders sagged. All he felt now was a deep sadness and extreme fatigue. He began to put on his asbestos gear.

"You're going back to the fire?"

"Yes." He snapped his suit into place and picked up his headgear. "You'll be gone when I get back."

She said nothing, knowing she would not be gone. He took her silence for acquiescence.

"Good-bye, Rachel."

"May the wind be beneath your wings, Jacob."

His head snapped back around, and they exchanged a long, deep look. Then he was gone.

Rachel dressed quickly after Jacob had left. She found some oatmeal packets and made herself a small breakfast. Not that she was hungry. In fact, the thought of food almost made her sick, but she knew she had to keep up her strength to fight Jacob. And that's exactly what she intended to do. She'd fight Jacob Donovan every step of the way. She'd fight his anger, his accusations, his false beliefs. She'd battle with him until she won. This was not about Benjy anymore. They'd settle that peacefully. Rachel was fighting for love now. The prize she wanted to win was Jacob Donovan himself. This time, she vowed fiercely, she wouldn't let him go.

She was washing her cereal bowl in the small sink when the door opened. The man who came through was blond and lean and handsome. He stopped just inside the door when he saw her.

"Pardon me. I didn't know anyone was here."

"I'm Rachel Devlin." She watched him closely when she told her name. He knew of her. She could tell by the play of emotions on his face. She decided that curiosity was the dominant emotion.

"Rick McGill, Jacob's right-hand man and friend." He came into the room and walked straight to a chair. "You don't mind if I sit down, do you? It's been a hell of a night."

His smile was quick and easy. Rachel liked him.

"Please do, Rick. I'd like to get to know you." She sat down opposite him.

Rick leaned across the table, his brown eyes intent. "Let's not pretend with each other, Rachel. I don't know you, but I know about you, and I know that Jacob is going through the tortures of the damned. He's my friend. Although you're a beautiful woman with a charming smile, I'll reserve judgment about whether you and I can be friends."

"Fair enough. Do you mind if I tell you a long story?"

He quirked one eyebrow upward. "Justification?"

"No. Only rationalization."

Pushing his chair back, he reached for the box of oatmeal. "I'll eat while you talk. And I have only twenty minutes."

At the end of twenty minutes Rachel had gained a friend.

"It's not my place to judge right or wrong, Rachel. And I believe you when you say you love Jacob."

"I *do*, Rick. And I'll go through hell to convince him of that."

"That's about where he is right now, Rachel. When I go back, we're going to set the explosives."

"Explosives!"

"It will be an attempt to use all the oxygen that's keeping the fire supplied. We'll set the charges as close to the wellhead as possible."

"Won't it be dangerous?"

"Everything we do is dangerous." Rick gave her a jaunty smile. "Even life is dangerous."

"I'm going with you."

"You can't. The area is sealed."

"Can you get me close enough to watch? If anything happened to Jacob, I'd blame myself. He's terribly tired, and he has a lot on his mind. I have to see him through this."

Rick made one of the snap decisions he was famous for.

"I'll get Jack's suit for you. He's on a sleep shift right now. And you'll do *exactly* as I tell you. Deal?"

She smiled. "Deal."

Dressed in an asbestos suit that bagged around her, Rachel was escorted to a small office building on the fringes of the oil field. Rick introduced her to the foreman and two members of the drilling crew who had been watching the progress of the fire-fighting team from the relative safety of the office.

"Don't move from this spot," Rick warned Rachel. "No matter what happens, you stay here."

Rachel took his hand. "Thank you, Rick. And good luck."

"That always helps." Rick donned his headgear and went toward the blazing wellhead.

Rachel stood beside the window, trying to pick out Jacob. From the distance, all the members of the fire-fighting team looked alike. In their suits and headgear, they resembled identical abominable snowmen. Sooty snowmen, she corrected herself. She'd just have to watch them all.

Suddenly one of the men separated himself from the crowd. He pulled off his headgear, and Rachel saw the flaming red hair. All the love she felt for Jacob welled up inside her heart, and she pressed close to the window, straining to get a better look.

Rick McGill joined Jacob. They put their heads

together in earnest conversation, and then Jacob picked up a large bundle.

"Explosives," Rachel whispered. She began to pray silently.

Jacob was moving back toward the burning well-head. Rachel watched and prayed. A thousand horrible images crowded her mind as Jacob courted death. Suddenly he was up and running. A thunderous explosion shook the small building where Rachel was. Flying debris and smoke obscured her vision for a moment. Then, through the mists she saw Jacob. He stumbled and fell. Chunks of flame rained around him.

"Jacob!" She was screaming, running. Hands clutched at her. Voices yelled at her to stop, but she kept on running. She had to get to Jacob.

She fought her way through the smoke, screaming his name. "Jacob!"

He rolled, cursing his lack of concentration and his own stupid fatigue. And then he heard her. Rachel. Terror clutched at him. Through the billowing smoke he could see her running toward him, still crying his name.

"Get back, dammit! Go back!" He was up on his feet, stumbling toward her. A chunk of flying metal fell into his path and he went down again.

Rachel bent over him. He reached out and jerked her down beside him as another fiery airborne missile landed close-by.

"Keep down," he yelled. "Duck your head and run with me."

He moved in a crouch, protecting Rachel with his arms and dragging her with him. Even under the headgear, she choked. Panic kept her on her feet—that and Jacob's arm wrapped securely around her.

They ran for what seemed to be an eternity, then suddenly they were in the clear.

Jacob threw his headgear off and reached for Rachel's. When he could see her face, he exploded.

"You could have been killed out there."

She faced his wrath with her head held high. "So could you."

"It's part of my job."

Rick came running toward them. "Jacob, what in hell happened out there?"

Keeping an iron grip on Rachel's arm, he turned toward his friend.

"My timing was off."

"Thank God, you're all right." Rick's face was pale under the layer of soot. "Good news, though. It looks like the explosives have done the trick." He clapped Jacob on the arm. "The next time, I'll go in. You're getting too old for this, buddy."

Jacob grinned. "Watch it, McGill. You're treading on thin ice." He glanced at Rachel's pale face. "Rachel, will you wait for me in the office? Rick and I have a few more things to do."

"I'll wait."

She started to leave, and Jacob caught her arm. "Are you all right?"

"Just a little shaken. I'll be fine. You go ahead and do your job, Jacob."

He watched her leave. She looked small and vulnerable in the too-big fire-fighting suit. But her chin was up and her step was firm.

"Don't be too hard on her, Jacob. I'm the one responsible for her being here."

Jacob spun back around. "You let her come?"

"I have a soft spot for women, and she can be very persuasive."

Jacob reined in his temper. He knew all too well Rachel's persuasive powers. Hadn't he been caught in her trap just last night? The bittersweet memory seared through him, and he ached with remorse.

He put his arm around Rick's shoulder. "It's okay, pal. I'd have done the same thing. Now, let's check this wellhead."

They inspected the site together. Their dramatic and dangerous plan had worked. The oxygen that had been supplying the fire had been used up by the explosives, and no more sparks were around to ignite the gas that still spewed from the well.

Jacob called his team and the drilling crew in to seal the wellhead. Rick pulled him aside.

"I can handle it from here, Jacob. Go to her."

"You're sure?"

"Absolutely. And Jacob . . . don't be too hard on her. She really does love you."

Jacob didn't trust himself to reply to that statement. Right now, he didn't even trust himself to think about love. The only thing he knew for certain was that he had to get Rachel out of Maracaibo. He didn't want her this close to danger; he didn't want ever to be as scared for her as he had been today.

She ran to him when he opened the door of the office. "Oh, lord, Jacob. You could have been killed." Her fingers were gentle as she caressed his face. "I just want to see for myself that you're in one piece."

He steeled himself against the tender feelings her touch always evoked in him. "I'm taking you out of here, Rachel. This is no place for a woman."

"I'm not just any woman, Jacob. I'm a woman in love. And I'm determined to fight for you."

He covered her hands with his and looked into her

eyes. "It's over between us, Rachel. The only thing we have in common now is Benjy."

"You say that because you're hurting. You'll change your mind. I'll *make* you change your mind."

His smile was bittersweet. "Do you know how gorgeous you are when you're fighting?" The urge to kiss her was strong in him. To keep from following through, he turned toward the door, keeping a hold on her hand. "Let's get out of here. We both need a shower."

They got into Jacob's Jeep and drove in silence to the small shack. Jacob sat at the table while Rachel showered away the black grime that was a part of every fire-fighter's life. She came out clean and shining, her wet hair slicked down.

She was so beautiful, she made him ache. He wanted to bury himself in her sweet flesh, to use her as a healing balm, to let her wipe away the harshness of his job. Instead he showered. The tepid water cleaned his body and helped clear his mind.

Dressed in clean jeans and shirt, he faced Rachel. "I told you to leave this morning."

She smiled at him. "Have you forgotten so much about me, Jacob? I rarely do what I'm told."

"I forgot this morning, and look what happened. You were almost killed. I won't make that mistake again." He left the table and got her gown off the bed, then he snapped open her bag and shoved it in.

"What do you think you're doing?"

"Packing your bag. Did you bring a toothbrush?"

"I'll do my own packing when I'm ready to leave— and I'm not ready to leave."

"Yes, you are. And to make damned sure that you do, I'm taking you to the airport and personally putting you on the plane."

"You are the most stubborn, high-handed, illogical, maddening. . . ."

"Why, Rachel. All this time you've been telling me how wonderful I am. Change your mind?"

His light, teasing tone was reminiscent of the old Jacob. Almost, but not quite. There were deep hurts that had to heal, and she was wise enough to know that time was her ally.

"All right, Jacob. I'll go. But I promise you—it's not over between us."

Ten

The first hour of the drive back to Maracaibo was the longest Rachel had ever endured. Jacob drove the Jeep without speaking, and she watched the scenery along the side of the road. The silence between them was uneasy. Never had it been like that with the two of them.

As they passed through a small village, she saw two barefoot boys alongside the road, tugging on a hemp rope. A reluctant goat was at the other end of the rope. The battle raged hot and heavy, and it looked as if the goat was winning.

"Look, Jacob. Let's stop and help them."

"Us or me?"

"Would I offer help if I didn't mean it?"

"You're on, Rachel." He pulled the Jeep off the side of the road. "But don't think this changes a thing. I'm still taking you to the airport, even if it takes all night."

Jacob's Spanish was excellent. He found out that the goat had escaped, and the boys were trying to get him back into his pen. They pointed out the pen just down the hill. When Jacob offered to help, they rolled their eyes and giggled.

"All right, Rachel. You said you wanted to help. I'll pull and you push."

"No. I'll pull and you push. I don't want to be at that end of the goat."

Jacob chuckled. The young boys asked for a translation, and when Jacob told them what she had said, they fell into the dirt, kicking their heels into the air and laughing.

Rachel tugged at the goat's rope, and Jacob shoved him from behind. But the stubborn old billy dug his heels in and refused to budge.

"This is not working, Jacob."

"Do you have a better idea?"

"Why don't we try talking to him?"

"Do you speak goat?"

"No, but I've never known a male animal who could resist my charm."

She caught the twinkle in Jacob's eye when she leaned and started cajoling the goat. Good, she thought. Her old Jacob was shining through.

"It's not working, Rachel."

"I'm not finished yet." Throwing back her head, she started to yodel. The billy goat's ears quivered, then he lowered his head and took a step toward her. Rachel started down the hill toward the goat pen. The goat tramped along behind her. Suddenly he got into the spirit of the song. Lowering his head, he nudged Rachel with his horns.

She started running, still yodeling, the goat hot on her trail.

"I'm coming, Rachel. Hang in there, kid." Jacob

sprinted down the hill after them, laughing so hard, he could hardly see.

For a while it was nip and tuck as to who was being herded into the pen. By the time Jacob got to the bottom of the hill, the billy was safely behind bars, and Rachel was leaning against the fence, laughing.

"What took you so long, Jacob?"

"I was enjoying the show. I didn't know you yodeled."

"I can do anything I set my mind to—including getting you back."

"After seeing the way you handled that stubborn goat, I should be trembling in my boots."

"Are you?"

"Nothing scares me."

After they got back into the Jeep, there was a sort of camaraderie between them. Rachel took advantage of the changed atmosphere to talk.

"You know, today is the first time I've seen you fighting an oil field fire."

"Were you afraid?"

"Yes, but it was different from the way I used to imagine it."

"How is that?"

"When I discovered I was pregnant and you were in Saudi Arabia, all I could think of was you at the mercy of the fire. I couldn't face that, Jacob. The thought of my child having no father terrified me."

She saw his jaw tighten, but he said nothing.

"Today I saw that it's not like that. *You* were the master, not the fire. Of course the danger is there, but you were the one in control."

"Funny how our timing always seems to be off,

isn't it, Rachel? If you had said that six years ago
. . ." His shrug was eloquent.

She reached over and touched his hand. "I'm so
sorry, Jacob."

"So am I."

"Forgive me."

He turned toward her, and his smile was sad.
"You ask more than I can give."

Jacob saw Rachel safely onto the homebound plane,
then he returned to his work. Within three days, he
and his team had completed the job they'd set out to
do. The plane was loaded with all their heavy fire-
fighting equipment.

He and his men celebrated at a small nightclub in
Maracaibo. The singer was dark skinned, dark eyed,
and sultry instead of blond and elegant, but she still
reminded him of Rachel. All her songs were fast-
paced Spanish numbers rather than slow blues songs,
but still she reminded him of Rachel. Everything
reminded him of Rachel—the full moon, the hot
sleepless nights, the sound of a woman's laughter,
the elusive scent of flowers that hung over the
city.

"Jacob."

"What?" Cradling his bottle of beer, he turned
toward Rick.

"Where were you, pal? We've asked you twice if
you're staying down here a few days with the rest of
us."

"No. I have an old friend in Panama. I think I'll
make a short hop there, then I'll take the equipment
on home. You can keep the Mustang down here."

Rick reached out and squeezed his shoulder. "Luck, Jacob."

"Thanks, Rick."

Jacob left Maracaibo in the early morning light. Lifting the plane upward toward the dawn, he waited for the soaring feeling of freedom that always accompanied his flights. For the first time in his memory, nothing happened. He was merely a tired man flying home to the States.

As he winged his way through the clouds, he thought of Rachel—that certain tilt of her head when she laughed, the throaty way she sang. Funny that his first thoughts were of her and not of his son, he thought. Strange that his heart still behaved as if he were in love.

He forced his mind away from thoughts of Rachel. The clouds were heavy today, the sky dark and troublesome. They matched his mood. His mind registered his checkpoint, and he glanced briefly at his watch.

As Jacob approached the Andes, he heard Rachel's voice. "I'm here for you, Jacob. I'll always be here for you." How paltry the words seemed when weighed against action. She'd denied him Benjy. And yet, she'd come to Maracaibo; she'd even risked her life.

Suddenly an awful silence descended on the plane. His radio was dead, and somewhere through those clouds lay the Andes Mountains. Under ordinary circumstances, Jacob would have climbed higher so that he could clear the peaks, but he was flying with a heavy load, all the fire-fighting equipment. There was no way the overloaded jet could clear the tops of the Andes. And he didn't have enough fuel to turn around and go back. He'd planned to make his first stop to refuel in Panama.

Adrenaline flowed through him, giving him that extra burst of energy he needed to face the danger. He knew that he had to make a ninety degree turn in order to go around the peaks, but he'd counted on radio contact to guide him. He strained forward, trying to see through the thick clouds. There was nothing in front of him except murky grayness—and possible death.

He'd flirted with death many times, but he'd never come face to face with it. Death in the mountains would be quick and relatively painless—one moment of bright, searing pain and then nothing. Oblivion. The agony of the last few days would be over. But so would life. Suddenly Jacob realized just how much he wanted to live. Everything he held precious existed in the real world—his son, his parents, his brothers and sisters and their families. And Rachel. In that clear moment, with death looming ahead, he knew that he still loved Rachel.

Sweat popped out on his brow, and he looked at his watch. He'd been in the air for over an hour, and he knew the mountains were close.

Jacob pitted all his skills against the dark mountains ahead. If he could remember the precise time he'd passed the last checkpoint, he could calculate the exact time he should make his turn. He closed his eyes briefly, forcing himself to relax. With great concentration, he cleared his mind of everything except flying. He couldn't afford any guessing games. He had only one move to make, and that had to be the right one.

Bit by bit he traced backward. He'd looked at his watch when he'd passed the checkpoint, but he hadn't been thinking of the time: he'd been thinking of how long it would be until he got home. He closed his eyes again, visualizing the dial, trying to create a precise image of the hands. Seven fifteen. The numbers sprang out at him. It had been 7:15 A.M. when he'd passed his checkpoint.

Jubilation filled him. He looked at his watch again. In exactly six minutes he had to make his turn. Jacob had been six minutes from death.

He made his turn at the appointed time and came out on the other side of the Andes. On this side of the mountains, the clouds had lifted. Bright sunlight poured through the cockpit as if God were shining his benediction down on Jacob.

The magnificent power of freedom soared through him. He threw back his head and laughed aloud. He knew exactly what he was going to do: He wouldn't stop to see his friend after refueling in Panama— he'd fly straight home to Rachel.

Four days after she'd left Maracaibo, Rachel was humming around her house in Biloxi.

Vashti put down her dust cloth, propped her hands on her hips, and scowled.

"I don't see what you have to be so cheerful about. After Jacob put you on that plane and sent you home, it seems to me you'd be trying to think of ways to get him back instead of flitting around here humming."

"That's exactly what I'm doing, Vashti. I'm scheming to win him back."

"Well, you sure could've fooled me. You've been

doing nothing for the last few days except preening
and primping, getting your nails done and having
your facials and letting that fruitcake mess with
your hair."

Rachel laughed. "He didn't mess with my hair; he
trimmed it."

"Ha. I liked it better the old way."

"Half an inch, Vashti. Who in the world misses
half an inch?"

"Jacob would—if he were here, and it looks to me
like that's been ruined. It seems to me we'll be mighty
lucky to ever see hide or hair of him again."

"He'll be here, and when he comes, I'll be ready for
him." She hummed another snatch of song.

"You better be eating some humble pie instead of
going around here humming. What is that infernal
song, anyhow?"

" 'Waltzing Matilda.' " Rachel took Vashti's arm
and led her toward the kitchen. "It's time for a tea
break, and while we're drinking, I'm going to tell you
something that will wipe that scowl off your face."

"I'm not scowling. I never scowl."

Rachel prepared two tall glasses of iced tea with
plenty of lemon and sugar, just the way Vashti liked
it, then she joined her surrogate mother at the kitchen
table.

"Once Jacob told me something about himself,
and I didn't remember it until I was back home in
Biloxi."

"Hmmmm." Vashti sipped her tea, unconvinced
that anybody could know more about Jacob Donovan than she did.

"He loves the unattainable. That's one attraction
flying has for him. Only the truly courageous dare to
attain the freedom of the skies."

Vashti thumped her tea glass on the table. "So what does that have to do with getting him back?"

Rachel grinned. "When he comes to Biloxi—and I know he will—I'm going to be unattainable."

Jacob stayed in Greenville only long enough to unload and service the jet, then he climbed into the Baron and headed for Biloxi. It was evening when he checked into the Broadwater Beach Hotel, and he was tired. But he didn't want to rest. He had to see Rachel. One quick call let him know that she was back at the club, singing two shows a night.

He went to the late show. She wasn't onstage when he slipped into his seat in a quiet corner near the back. He ordered a drink and waited, tense and expectant.

When she walked onstage, he forgot to breathe. She was shining and glorious, as if she were the finest plane in the world and had been buffed and polished with a chamois cloth. She was wearing a shimmery gown of iridescent beads that moved when she did and shot sparks of fire. Jacob couldn't wait to get his hands on her.

She saw him. He could tell by the shine in her eyes and the high color on her cheeks. Smiling, he leaned back in his seat and listened to her sing. It was a slow, pulsing blues number, and she sang it to him. In fact, she sang all her numbers to him. It was so obvious that heads turned to look in his direction. The curious nightclub patrons wanted to see the object of all Rachel Devlin's attention.

Jacob loved the attention. He acknowledged all the knowing smiles and curious glances with a wicked, devil-may-care smile.

Onstage Rachel was relieved. She hadn't known what his mood would be when he came to Biloxi, but his smile had told her everything. There was no tension, no anger in him. Apparently time had been a healer.

Giving a silent prayer of thanks, she turned all her persuasive powers on him. With body language and sultry voice, she made it abundantly clear that she was singing only for him. Watching his reaction, she was secretly delighted. She had Jacob Donovan thinking she'd fall into his lap like a ripe plum. So much the better. He'd be caught completely off guard.

After the show was over, Rachel went to her dressing room and waited. She didn't have to wait long. Jacob gave one commanding knock, then he pushed open her door. He'd tried to tame his hair but hadn't succeeded. It looked like a wild red halo around his face. The spark in his blue eyes was so bright, she wondered why the room didn't catch fire.

"Hello, Jacob." He never lost his smile. Her coolness hadn't registered on him yet.

"Rachel." He moved into the room as if he owned it.

She sat at her dressing table and picked up her hairbrush. She would use every weapon at her disposal, and she knew what the sight of her brushing her hair did to Jacob Donovan. As she pulled the brush through her mass of hair, she watched the effect the action was having. A muscle jumped in Jacob's cheek, and he moved abruptly to a chair. He gripped the chair back so hard his knuckles turned white.

"I suppose you're here to talk about Benjy." Rachel leaned over and brushed her hair from the underside. She had to do something to hide the gloating look on her face.

"Actually, I'm not. What I have in mind will solve any problems we might have had over our son."

"Our son?"

"Yes, Rachel. Yours and mine."

"In Maracaibo he was *your* son."

"You have every right to be upset with me."

She put her hairbrush on the dressing table and stood up. With languorous movements, she lifted her hair off the back of her neck and stretched. She hoped the move shot his blood pressure up ten notches.

Letting her hair drift back through her fingers, she smiled at him. "I'm not upset, Jacob. You were exactly right. Benjy is your son, too, and we'll work out the details like two sane, sensible adults. There's no need to let past feelings enter into this discussion."

"Past feelings?"

"Yes."

"In Maracaibo, you said you loved me."

"And you said you didn't love me. I accept that." She turned her back to him. "Will you help me with this zipper, Jacob? I need to get out of this dress."

Jacob didn't move. "If I take you out of that dress, we'll be here the rest of the night, and it won't be to change clothes." Suddenly he bolted from his chair and caught her shoulders. "Dammit, Rachel. Look at me."

She turned slowly around. He was standing so close, she could feel his body heat. She almost abandoned her game. Forcing herself to ignore her passion, she looked straight into Jacob's eyes. He had to know that she was his match. By her actions she had to show him that he couldn't walk away from her love and then win her over with a smile.

"I'm looking, Jacob. You look tired. You should have taken a week or two to rest."

Jacob could hardly believe what he was hearing. A few minutes ago he'd have sworn she was singing those love songs especially for him, and now she was acting as though he barely existed.

"I had other things on my mind."

"Benjy."

"No. You."

"I suppose you want to give me a few more orders. It won't work."

"I'm not here to give you orders, Rachel. I'm here to tell you that I love you."

Until she heard him say the words, she hadn't been certain. Her relief was so great, it made her weak. Keeping her face expressionless, she reached out and patted his cheek.

"I'll bet you say that to all the girls."

"Dammit, Rachel. What is the matter with you? You came down to Maracaibo to ask for my forgiveness and my love. I'm telling you now that I forgive you and that I love you. What in the hell is wrong?"

"Why should I believe you? What makes this time any different from the last time? You carried me up in that plane and declared you'd always love me, and then what did you do? When I got to Maracaibo—to tell you the truth, by the way, and don't you ever forget that—when I got down there, you treated me like a complete stranger." She stalked around the room, every step and gesture calculated to show off her body in the revealing gown she'd chosen so carefully. Heartless, she thought with glee. That's what she was.

Jacob caught her around the waist and pulled her against his chest. "I don't make love to complete strangers."

She arched her eyebrows. "Is that what that was, Jacob? Love?"

"Yes. I'll admit I was a jackass. I took the truth badly. But I've never touched you except in the name of love." He let his hands trail slowly down her back. "Coming home, I realized that I'd never stopped loving you. I can never stop, Rachel. You're the other half of my heart."

She tipped her head back and smiled. "I'll admit I want you, Jacob. Sex was always good between us. But that's not love." Easing out of his arms, she reached behind her back and pulled down her zipper. "You can leave now. I'm going to undress and go home."

His gaze burned over her. For a moment, she thought he was going to say something else, and then he turned on his heel and left.

She sank into her chair and put her head on her dressing table. If Jacob Donovan had known how close she was to losing control, he would never have left, she decided. One more minute, two at the most, and she'd have been in his arms begging to be loved.

She stood up and dressed quickly. Tonight was only round one. Tomorrow would be another day, and she needed her rest.

The next day, Jacob's note arrived. "Dear Rachel," it read, "let's have dinner together before your early show. I'll pick you up at six. Love, Jacob." A single white rose was attached.

Smiling and humming, she put the rose in water and carried it upstairs to her bedroom. Then she picked up the telephone and called Jacob.

"I got your note and the rose. Thanks."

"I knew you'd like the rose. Is six too early for you?"

"The time doesn't matter. I can't go with you tonight."

"Other plans, Rachel?"

"My plans are none of your concern. Good-bye, Jacob."

She knew Jacob wouldn't give up. And she was right. Two hours after the phone call, Vashti called her out into the front yard.

"What is it, Vashti?"

"Wait a minute. He'll come back."

"Who?"

"Jacob. Benjy and I were practicing his curve ball, and Benjy saw it first. He showed it to me before he went inside for cookies."

Rachel laughed. "Do you know that you drive me crazy? Stark raving mad. What in this world are you talking about?"

"If I told you it wouldn't be a surprise." Vashti stopped talking and grabbed Rachel's arm. "Look. Up yonder in the sky."

It was a jet, flying fast and low. As Rachel watched, the plane began to do a series of loops and curves. The contrail spelled I LOVE YOU, RACHEL.

"He's going to kill himself, Vashti. He's not a stunt flyer."

"How do you know that's him up there? Maybe he hired somebody else to do the job."

"I know, Vashti. I know."

She shaded her eyes and watched the plane pass over her house and come back. I LOVE YOU, RACHEL appeared in the sky once more, then the vapor broke apart and disappeared.

"You crazy, wonderful man. I love you too," she whispered.

Vashti smiled.

Late that afternoon, Jacob called her. He made no mention of the airplane stunt, and neither did she.

"Since you're busy tonight, I thought I'd stake my claim for tomorrow night. Before or after your show."

"I'm sorry, Jacob. I can't."

"That's okay. The night after will do."

"Sorry again."

"I suppose you're going to tell me you're otherwise engaged for the next two weeks."

She laughed. "Of course not. I never make plans more than two nights in advance."

"Is that something new with you, Rachel?"

"It could be, Jacob. There are a lot of things you don't know about me anymore."

"One way or the other, I intend to find out. Good-bye, Rachel."

Jacob came to her club that night, but he left without coming backstage. She'd expected another confrontation. In fact, she'd counted on it. When she left the club, she was so upset, she got stopped for speeding on the way home. And she hadn't even realized she was going fast.

"Your driver's license, please."

She prided herself on knowing most of the police force because they were big fans of hers. But this officer was new. What the heck, she thought. She'd try to charm him anyway. She hated fines with a passion, and she'd use any ploy to get out of one.

"You caught me red-handed, Officer. I hope you won't be too hard on me." She gave him a smile she hoped was devastating, and she even batted her eyelashes at him. She hoped lightning didn't strike her dead for her shameless ways.

He was not impressed. He checked her license, then turned his flashlight onto her face. "Rachel Devlin, are you?"

"Yes. I'm the singer." She smiled again, but the officer was still not overwhelmed. She decided she'd lost her touch. Leaning out her window, she read his badge. "Officer Richards . . . can I be frank with you?"

He grinned. "You might try that instead of flirting."

"Flirting?"

"Yeah. All that fluttering and simpering. I've got a wife and six kids. I'm immune—even to a good-looking dame like you."

"I'm a little frustrated tonight, and I really wasn't paying attention to the speedometer. Man trouble."

He leaned down to get a closer look at her face. "Not abuse, is it?"

"Oh, no. Nothing like that. It's just love. We can't seem to get things right. First he's willing and I'm not, then I am and he's not. It's very complicated."

"Love always is." Officer Richards handed her driver's license back to her. "Under the circumstances I'm going to let you off with a warning. Take it easy."

"In the car or in the love battle?"

"Both."

He tipped his hat and left.

Rachel drove at a snail's pace all the way home. She saw the shadow on her porch the minute she swung into her driveway. Her foot hit the brake, and her hand reached for the spray bottle of ammonia under her front seat. While she was trying to decide whether to turn around and drive for help or whether to attack the intruder with her household ammonia, he stepped into the light. His red hair lit up like a flame.

She rolled down the window. "Jacob, you scared me half to death."

"What took you so long, Rachel?"

"First my zipper got stuck and I had to get Louie to get me out of my dress, then I got stopped for speeding. I tried flirting and nearly got arrested for trying to bribe an officer. And then you show up on my front porch. Jacob Donovan, I could kill you."

He roared with laughter. "Can you wait until after the concert, love? I couldn't play too well as a corpse."

"What concert? It's nearly three o'clock in the morning. Are you crazy?"

"I'm crazy in love." He opened the door on the driver's side and scooted her over. "And so are you. Since you're so busy avoiding me, I decided the only way to get this thing settled is to kidnap you." He drove the car smoothly into the garage and locked the doors. Then he turned to face her. "It took me a while to figure it out, Rachel. And I'll have to tell you that I'm impressed. You show remarkable spunk for a woman your age."

"A woman my age. What does that have to do with anything?"

"A woman your age should be married and having kids."

"Jacob Donovan, wipe that smirk off your face. I'm tired and I'm going to bed."

"*We* certainly are. As soon as we get this settled."

He lifted her onto his lap and pulled out his harmonica.

"What in the world are you doing?"

"This afternoon, after you'd turned down all my invitations, it occurred to me that you wanted to be courted. You're playing hard to get, Rachel." He grinned at her. "You knew I wouldn't be able to resist it, didn't you?"

"I'll reserve my answer until I hear this concert. I'm not easily won, you know."

"I know." He put the harmonica to his lips and began to play his song. Even when he missed the B-flat, the music was soft and hauntingly beautiful in the car. Rachel began to sing along.

When it was over, she pressed her head against his shoulder. He brushed his lips against her temple.

"Will you come awaltzing with me, Rachel?" His teasing tone was gone, and his voice was so tender, it made her throat ache.

"Where, Jacob?"

"To the altar."

"You want to get married?"

"I've wanted you to be my wife since the first day I saw you. Fate has delayed us a while, but I think we can make up for lost time."

"We'll fight a lot, Jacob."

"Making up will be fun."

"I still don't really *like* flying."

"As long as you like me."

"Sometimes I'm grouchy in the morning."

"I have a cure."

"And in the winter my feet get cold. I've been known to wear socks to bed."

"I'll keep you warm."

She cupped his face. "Will you love me, Jacob?" she asked fiercely. "Will you love me always, and not ever, ever let me go?"

"I'll never let you go again, Rachel. I've lost you twice. I don't intend for that to happen again." He kissed her softly, then leaned back to look into her eyes. "Can you live with my profession, my sweet?"

"Yes. I'm stronger than I used to be. I found that out in Maracaibo."

"I want Benjy to bear my name. How do you feel about that?"

Her smile was tender. "From the day he could walk, he's wanted to fly. He's always been a Donovan at heart. We might as well make it legal." She leaned closer, searching his face in the dark. "Are you sure the past is behind us, Jacob? Have you forgiven me?"

"Yes. My heart forgave you from the moment I knew Benjy was my son. It just took my mind a little while to catch up. Will you marry me, Rachel?"

"Yes. But will you do something for me, first?"

"Anything."

"Play that song again. I think it's the most beautiful song in the world."

"And afterward?"

"You won't think I'm easy if I say this?"

"Try me."

She smiled. "How do you feel about making out in the car?"

"I can handle that."

Epilogue

"Look at that, Rachel." Jacob bent his face close to the tiny bundle he was holding. "He knows me already. See how he's smiling?"

"That's gas, Jacob. All babies have gas." Rachel stood in the doorway of the nursery and watched her husband dote on their infant son. It was a memory she would cherish forever.

"Nonsense. All the Donovans are smart. Do you think it's too soon to start filling out his application to Vanderbilt?"

"There's one little thing we should do first."

"What's that?"

"Feed him. Otherwise he'll misbehave at his own christening." She took the baby from Jacob and leaned down to croon into his sweet face. "We can't have that now, can we, little one?"

Jacob leaned over Rachel's shoulder and watched his son nurse. The sight made him misty eyed. He began to hum "Waltzing Matilda," off-key. Outside, the March winds, singing over the Mississippi

River, seemed to keep in tune. The sounds of a child playing drifted through the house. Benjy, Jacob thought, making the house in Greenville a home with his laughter.

Suddenly a little bright-eyed face peeped around the nursery-room doorway.

"Daddy?"

Jacob hurried to his oldest son. Squatting down so he would be on Benjamin's level, he put his arm around the boy's small shoulders. "What is it, son?"

"Vashti says for Joe to hurry up, or we'll be late to the church. Can you fix my bow tie? It got whopsided."

All the Donovans were waiting at the church for the christening of Jacob's son—all the Donovans except Tanner. He'd called from Dallas that morning to offer his congratulations and to ask Rachel how to tie hair ribbons. He was trying to dress his two daughters so they'd look gorgeous to welcome their baby brothers home from the hospital. Six days earlier Amanda had given birth to triplets.

As Jacob and Rachel walked down the aisle with their two sons, he looked at his family. His mother, Anna, didn't look a day older than she had twenty years ago. Maybe there was more silver in her hair, but her smile was just as young and gay. Matthew still stood as straight and tall as any of his sons, and he still had that devil-may-care spark in his eyes as he stood with his arm around Anna.

Charles, Glover, and Theo Donovan took up four pews with their large families. Charles even had a son-in-law and would soon be a grandfather.

Martie Donovan sat alone, for her husband, Reverend Paul Donovan, would be performing the christening ceremony. Martie was still the flamboyant beauty who had fallen out of the tree and into his brother's arms, Jacob thought. Her bangle bracelets tinkled softly as she pushed her long blond hair back from her face. She looked radiant, even in the last trimester of her pregnancy. The twins hadn't lost that angelic look, especially blond and beautiful Elizabeth, who was unmercifully poking her twin brother and punching her younger brother. Jacob almost laughed aloud. Looks were certainly deceiving.

His sister Hallie and her husband, Josh Butler, occupied the next pew. Still very much the scamp herself, she winked at Jacob as he walked down the aisle. She held her six-month-old son, and Josh cradled the head of their small daughter, who had fallen asleep in his arms, her golden hair fanning across his lap.

On down the aisle, Hannah had tears of joy in her eyes, for she of all Jacob's brothers and sisters, knew what his happiness had cost him. When Jacob passed the pew where she and her husband Jim Roman were sitting, he stopped to give her a quick hug. Her daughter with the dark gypsy hair and blue eyes, so like her mother, whispered, "Uncah Jacob, can I swap my baby brother for your baby? Britt squalls too much."

Across the aisle, Martin Windham chuckled. He had not only become reconciled to having Jacob for a son-in-law, but he'd been heard bragging around town that he had the handsomest, most intrepid Donovan of the lot as the father of his grandchildren. Nobody dared disagree with him.

Reverend Paul Donovan waited at the front of the church. Jacob stood proudly at the altar, holding Benjy with one hand and circling Rachel's waist with the other. The baby in her arms smiled in his sleep.

Paul opened his Bible and began the christening ceremony of Joseph Windham Donovan.

Afterward, cuddled together in the large bed that faced the river, Jacob whispered to his wife, "Do you think we might have another eight-month baby?"

"Let's try for nine this time, Jacob."

He smoothed back her hair and kissed her cheek.

"Jacob?"

"Hmmmm?"

"Fly with me."

"The Baron is in the hangar."

"We don't need a plane to fly."

Smiling, he shifted her under him. "I'm going to take you higher than eagles, my Rachel."

And he did.

THE EDITOR'S CORNER

This month we're inaugurating a special and permanent feature that is dear to our hearts. From now on we'll spotlight one Fan of the Month at the end of the Editor's Corner. Through the years we've enjoyed and profited from your praise, your criticisms, your analyses. So have our authors. We want to share the joy of getting to know a devoted romance reader with all of you other devoted romance readers—thus, this feature. We hope you'll enjoy getting to know our first Fan of the Month, Pat Diehl.

Our space is limited this month due to the addition of our new feature, so we can give you only a few tasty tidbits about each upcoming book.

Leading off is Kay Hooper with LOVESWEPT #360, **THE GLASS SHOE,** the second in her *Once Upon a Time* series. This modern Cinderella story tells the tale of beautiful heiress Amanda Wilderman and dashing entrepreneur Ryder Foxx, who meet at a masquerade ball. Their magical romance will enchant you, and the fantasy never ends—not even when the clock strikes midnight!

Gail Douglas is back with *The Dreamweavers*: **GAMBLING LADY,** LOVESWEPT #361, also the second in a series. Captaining her Mississippi riverboat keeps Stefanie Sinclair busy, but memories of her whirlwind marriage to Cajun rogue T.J. Carriere haunt her. T.J. never understood what drove them apart after only six months, but he vows to win his wife back. Stefanie doesn't stand a chance of resisting T.J.—and neither will you!

LOVESWEPT #362, **BACK TO THE BEDROOM** by Janet Evanovich, will have you in stitches! For months David Dodd wanted to meet the mysterious woman who was always draped in a black cloak and carrying a large, odd case—and he finally gets the chance when a helicopter drops a chunk of metal through his lovely neighbor's roof and he rushes to her rescue. Katherine Finn falls head over heels for David, but as a dedicated concert musician, she can't fathom the man who seems to be drifting through life. This wonderful story is sure to strike a chord with you!

Author Fran Baker returns with another memorable romance, **KING OF THE MOUNTAIN,** LOVESWEPT #363. Fran deals with a serious subject in **KING OF THE MOUNTAIN,** and she handles it beautifully. Heroine Kitty

(continued)

Reardon carries deep emotional scars from a marriage to a man who abused her, and hero Ben Cooper wants to offer her sanctuary in his arms. But Kitty is afraid to reach out to him, to let him heal her soul. This tenderly written love story is one you won't soon forget.

Iris Johansen needs no introduction, and the title of her next LOVESWEPT, #364, **WICKED JAKE DARCY,** speaks for itself. But we're going to tantalize you anyway! Mary Harland thinks she's too innocent to enchant the notorious rake Jake Darcy, but she's literally swept off her feet by the man who is temptation in the flesh. Dangerous forces are at work, however, forcing Mary to betray Jake and begin a desperate quest. We bet your hearts are already beating in double-time in anticipation of this exciting story. Don't miss it!

From all your cards and letters, we know you all just love a bad-boy hero, and has Charlotte Hughes got one for you in **SCOUNDREL,** LOVESWEPT #365. Growing up in Peculiar, Mississippi, Blue Mitchum had been every mother's nightmare, and every daughter's fantasy. When Cassie Kennard returns to town as Cassandra D'Clair, former world-famous model, she never expects to encounter Blue Mitchum again—and certainly never guessed he'd be mayor of the town! Divorced, the mother of twin girls, Cassie wants to start a new life where she feels safe and at home, but Blue's kisses send her into a tailspin! These two people create enough heat to singe the pages. Maybe we should publish this book with a warning on its cover!

Enjoy next month's LOVESWEPTs and don't forget to keep in touch!

Sincerely,

Carolyn Nichols

Carolyn Nichols
Editor
LOVESWEPT
Bantam Books
666 Fifth Avenue
New York, NY 10103

LOVESWEPT IS PROUD
TO INTRODUCE OUR FIRST
FAN OF THE MONTH

Pat Diehl

I was speechless when Carolyn Nichols called to say she wanted me to be LOVESWEPT's first **FAN OF THE MONTH,** but I was also flattered and excited. I've read just about every LOVESWEPT ever published and have corresponded with Carolyn for many years. I own over 5,000 books, which fill two rooms in my house. LOVESWEPT books are "keepers," and I try to buy them all and even get them autographed. Sometimes I reread my favorites—I've read **LIGHTNING THAT LINGERS** by Sharon and Tom Curtis twenty-seven times! Some of my other favorite authors are Sandra Brown, Joan Elliott Pickart, Billie Green, and Mary Kay McComas, but I also enjoy reading the new authors' books.

Whenever I come across a book that particularly moves me, I buy a copy, wrap it in pretty gift paper, and give it to a senior citizen in my local hospital. I intend to will all my romance books to my granddaughter, who's now two years old. She likes to sit next to me and hold the books in her hands as if she were reading them. It's possible that there could be another **FAN OF THE MONTH** in the Diehl family in the future!